PELICAN BOOKS

THE ROMANS

THE ROMANS

R. H. BARROW

WITH SO MANY TEACHERS AND WITH SO MANY
EXAMPLES HAS ANTIQUITY FURNISHED US THAT
NO AGE CAN BE THOUGHT MORE FORTUNATE IN
THE CHANCE OF ITS BIRTH THAN OUR OWN AGE,
FOR WHOSE INSTRUCTION MEN OF EARLIER GENE-
RATIONS HAVE EARNESTLY LABOURED.

QUINTILIAN (A.D. 35–95)

PENGUIN BOOKS

PENGUIN BOOKS

Published by the Penguin Group
27 Wrights Lane, London W8 5TZ, England
Viking Penguin Inc., 40 West 23rd Street, New York, New York 10010, USA
Penguin Books Australia Ltd, Ringwood, Victoria, Australia
Penguin Books Canada Ltd, 2801 John Street, Markham, Ontario, Canada L3R 1B4
Penguin Books (NZ) Ltd, 182–190 Wairau Road, Auckland 10, New Zealand

Penguin Books Ltd, Registered Offices: Harmondsworth, Middlesex, England

First published 1949
25 27 29 30 28 26

Printed and bound in Great Britain by
Cox & Wyman Ltd, Reading
Set in Intertype Baskerville

To
P. I. B.

Messrs Macmillan have kindly granted permission to quote a passage from J. W. Mackail's translation of the Aeneid of Virgil, Messrs G. Bell & Sons to quote from J. Conington's translation of Horace, and Messrs Heinemann to quote from M. Heseltine's translation of Petronius in the Loeb Classical Library. Grateful acknowledgement of this permission is made.

CONTENTS

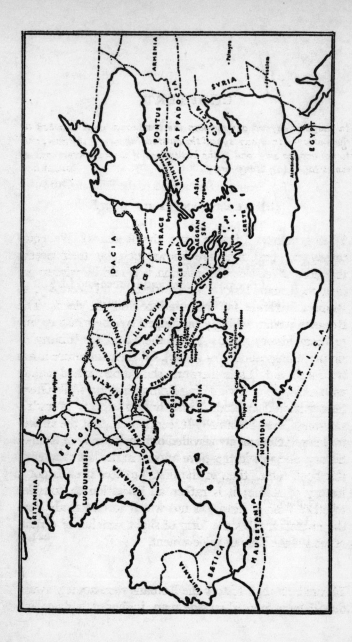

CHAPTER I

In the days beyond our memory the traditional ways attached to themselves by their own appeal the outstanding men of the time; and to the ancient ways and to the institutions of their ancestors men of moral superiority clung fast.   CICERO

(a) WHAT MANNER OF MEN?

WHAT manner of men were the Romans? We commonly say that men are known best by their deeds; therefore to answer this question it would be wise to go, first, to Roman history for the deeds, and, secondly, to Roman literature for the mind behind the deeds. The Romans would willingly be judged by their history, for to them history meant deeds; the Latin for 'history' is simply 'things done' (*res gestae*). Of their literature it has been well said, 'Latin literature should be studied mainly with a view to understanding Roman history, while Greek history should be studied mainly with a view to understanding Greek literature'. It seems, then, that the answer to the question can be provided only by a study of Roman history, and should therefore appear in the last chapter of this book rather than in the first. But this book is not a history of Rome; it is rather an invitation to consider whether Roman history is not worth further study, and the invitation takes the form of slight sketches of certain aspects of the Roman achievement.

*

Throughout their history the Romans were acutely aware that there is 'power' outside man, individually or collectively, of which man must take account. He must subordinate himself to something. If he refuses, he invites disaster; if he subordinates himself unwillingly, he becomes the victim of superior force; if willingly, he finds that he may be raised to the rank of cooperator; by cooperation he can see something of the trend, even the purpose, of that superior power. Willing cooperation gives a sense of dedication; the purposes become clearer, and he feels he is an agent or an instrument in forwarding them; at a higher level he becomes conscious of a vocation, of a mission for himself and for men like him, who compose the state. When the Roman general celebrated his 'triumph' after a victorious campaign, he progressed through the city from the gates to the temple of Jupiter (later in imperial times to the temple of Mars Ultor) and there offered to the god 'the achievements of Jupiter wrought *through* the Roman people'.

From the earliest days of Rome we can detect in the Roman a sense of dedication, at first crude and inarticulate and by no means unaccompanied by fear. In later days it is clearly expressed and is often a mainspring of action. In the latest days the mission of Rome is clearly proclaimed; it is often proclaimed most loudly by men who strictly were not Romans, and most insistently at the very time when in its visible expression the mission was accomplished. The sense of dedication at first reveals itself in humble forms, in the household and in the family; it is enlarged in the city-state and it finds its culmination in the imperial idea. From time to time it employs different categories of thought and modes of expression; but in its essence it is religious, for it is a leap beyond experience. When the mission is accomplished, its basis changes.

This is the clue to Roman character and to Roman history.

The Roman mind is the mind of the farmer and soldier; not farmer, nor soldier, but farmer–soldier; and this is true on the whole even in the later ages when the Roman might be neither farmer nor soldier. 'Unremitting work' is the lot of the farmer, for the seasons wait for no man. Yet his own work by itself will achieve nothing; he may plan and prepare, till and sow; in patience he must await the aid of forces which he cannot understand, still less control. If he can make them favourable, he will; but most often he can only cooperate, and he places himself in line with them that they may use him as their instrument, and so he may achieve his end. Accidents of weather and pest may frustrate him; he must accept compromise and be patient. Routine is the order of his life; seed-time, growth, and harvest follow in appointed series. The life of the fields is his life. If as a citizen he is moved to political action at last, it will be in defence of his land or his markets or the labour of his sons. To him the knowledge born of experience is worth more than speculative theory. His virtues are honesty and thrift, forethought and patience, work and endurance and courage, self-reliance, simplicity, and humility in the face of what is greater than himself.

Such also are the virtues of the soldier. He too will know the value of routine, which is a part of discipline, for he must respond as by instinct to a sudden call. He must be self-reliant. The strength and endurance of the farmer serve the soldier; his practical skill helps him to become what the Roman soldier must be, a builder and a digger of ditches and maker of roads and ramparts. He lays out a camp or a fortification as well as he lays out a plot or a system of drains. He can live on the land, for that is what he has done all his life. He too knows the incalculable element which may upset the best of dispositions. He is conscious of unseen forces, and he attributes 'luck' to a successful general whom some power – destiny or fortune – uses as an instrument. He gives his loyalty to persons and to places and to friends. If he becomes politically violent, he will be violent to secure, when the wars are over, land to till and a farm to live in; and still greater loyalty rewards the general who champions his cause. He has seen many men and many places, and with due caution he will imitate what he has seen to work; but for him 'that corner of the earth smiles above all others', his home and native fields, and he will not wish to see them changed.

The study of Roman history is, first, the study of the process by which Rome, always conscious of her dedication, painfully grew from being the city-state on the Seven Hills until she became mistress of the world; secondly, the study of the means by which she acquired and maintained that dominion; the means was her singular power of turning enemies into friends, and eventually into Romans, while yet they remained Spaniards or Gauls or Africans. From her they derived 'Romanitas', their 'Roman-ness'. 'Romanitas' is a convenient word used by the Christian Tertullian to mean all that a Roman takes for granted, the Roman point of view and habit of thought. It is akin to 'Roman civilization' only upon a strict view of what civilization is. Civilization is what men think and feel and do and the values which they assign to what they think and feel and do. It is true that their creative thoughts and their standards of feeling and value may issue in acts which profoundly affect the use which they make of material things; but 'material civilization' is the least important aspect of civilization, which really resides in men's minds. As Tacitus said, it is the ignorant (and he was speaking of the Britons) who think that fine buildings and

comforts and luxuries make up civilization. The Latin
word here used (*humanitas*) was a favourite word with
Cicero, and the conception behind it was peculiarly
Roman and was born of Roman experience. It means, on
the one side, the sense of the dignity of one's own human
personality, which is a thing unique and which must be
cared for and developed to the full; on the other side, it
means a recognition of the personalities of others and
their right to care for their own personalities; and this
recognition implies compromise and self-restraint and
sympathy and consideration.

But the usual and more concrete phrase for civilization
is simply 'the Roman peace'. It was in this idea that the
world found it easiest to see the fulfilment of that mission
which Roman character and experience and power had
gradually brought to the upper levels of consciousness and
had deliberately discharged. In the earliest days of the
Roman people its leader solemnly took the 'auspices' by
observation of signs revealed through religious rites, to
discover whether the action which the state proposed to
take was in line with the gods' will, which ruled the world.
Cicero, enumerating the fundamental principles upon
which the state rests, places first 'religion and the auspices',
and by 'auspices' he means that unbroken succession of
men from Romulus onwards to whom was given the duty
to discover the gods' will. The 'auspices' and the sacred
colleges, the Vestal Virgins and the rest, find their place in
the letters of Symmachus, born A.D. 340, who was a
tenacious leader of pagan opposition to Christianity, the
'official' religion of the Empire. Cicero it is who says that
the birth of Roman power, its increase and its maintenance, are due to Roman religion; Horace says that
subordination to the gods has given the Roman his
empire. Four centuries later St Augustine devotes the first

part of his most powerful book to wrestling with the prevalent faith that the greatness of Rome had been due to pagan gods, and that salvation from the threatening doom was to be found in them. It may well be said, in the words of the Greek Polybius, 205–123 B.C., himself a sceptic, 'What more than anything else distinguishes the Roman state and sets it above all others is its attitude to the gods. It seems to me that what is a reproach to other communities actually holds together the Roman state – I mean its awe of the gods', and he uses the same word which St Paul used on Mars' Hill in Athens. Polybius was not to know that at the very end, when the Roman Empire was overrun by barbarians, it would be the idea of the greatness and eternity of Rome which would hold together belief in the gods.

(b) 'THE OLD WAYS'

Roman religion was the religion, first of the family, then of the extension of the family, the state. The family was consecrate, so, therefore, was the state. The simple ideas and rites held and practised by families were adjusted and enlarged, partly by new conceptions created by new needs, partly by contact with other races and cultures, when families came together to form settlements and so eventually to fashion the city of Rome.

Anthropologists have given the name 'animism' to the stage of primitive religion which supposes a 'power' or 'spirit' or 'will' to reside in everything. To the primitive Roman, *numen*, power, or will, resided everywhere, or rather it manifested itself everywhere by action. All that can be known about it is that it acts, but the manner of its acting is undetermined. Man is an intruder into the realm of spirit, whose characteristic is action. How can he miti-

gate the awe which he feels, and how can he secure that
the *numen* shall produce the requisite action, and so win
for himself the 'peace of the gods'?

The first need is to 'fix' this vague power in a way
acceptable to it, and so to narrow or to focus its action
into this or that purpose vital to man. It was thought that
to *name* its manifestation in individual phenomena gave
definition to what was vague, and, so to speak, piped the
energy into the desired end. And so, as the actions of the
farmer and his family, engaged in agriculture and weaving
and cooking and bringing up children, were many, so the
activity of this power was split up into innumerable *named*
powers energizing the actions of the household. Every
minute operation of nature and man – the manifold life
of the fields, the daily tasks of the farmer, the daily round
of his wife, the growth and care of their children – took
place in the presence and by the energy of these vague
powers, now becoming formless deities.

With 'naming', i.e. invocation, went prayers and offerings of food and meal, milk and wine, and, on occasion,
animal sacrifice. The appropriate words and rites were
known to the head of the family, who was the priest.
Words and ritual were passed on from father to son till
they were fixed immutably. A flaw in invocation or ceremony would prevent the *numen* from issuing into the
action which the family or individual was undertaking,
and so failure would result. The names of many of these
household gods have passed into the languages of Europe:
Vesta, the spirit of the hearth-fire; the Penates, the pre-
servers of the store-cupboard; the Lares, the guardians of
the house. But there were very many others. Daily prayer
was said; the family meal was a religious ceremony, and
incense and libations were offered. Certain festivals related to the dead, who were sometimes regarded as hostile

and therefore to be expelled from the house by rite, som-
times as kindly spirits to be associated closely with all
family festivals and anniversaries.

When the families coalesced to form a community,
family cult and ritual formed the basis of state cult. At
first the king was the priest; when kings ceased to exist, the
title survived as 'king of the sacred things'. To help the
'king' were 'colleges' of priests, that is to say, ordinary
men, not a special caste, who were colleagues together in
ordering worship and festivals. The chief college was that
of the *pontifices*, which took charge of the accumulated
lore, made rules, and kept records of feasts and of outstanding events of religious significance to the state. They
built up a sacred law (*ius divinum*). Minor colleges
assisted them; thus, the Vestal Virgins tended the hearth-
fire of the state, the augurs took the omens from the flight
of birds or from the entrails of a sacrificed animal; for the
gods were supposed to impress on the sensitive organs of
a consecrated animal signs of approval or of disapproval.
The agricultural festivals of the farmstead were given
national importance; the harvest, the safety of the
boundaries, the hunting of wolves from the fields became
the concern of the city. New festivals were added, and the
list was kept in a Calendar, of which we have records. In
his origin Mars was a god of the fields; the farmer–
soldiers, organized for war, turned him into a god of battle.
New gods came to the notice of the Romans as their horizon widened; and deities of the Etruscan and Greek cities
in Italy found their way into the Calendar. Jupiter, Juno,
and Minerva came from Etruria; the Greek Hephaistos
was equated with Volcanus, whom the Romans took over
from their Etruscan neighbours. There were many 'Italic'
deities too, for, though we have spoken for simplicity's
sake of Romans, Rome was itself made up of a fusion of

Italic tribes with special cults of their own, no doubt bearing a certain family likeness.

The formulae of invocation and prayer were handed down and elaborated and recorded unchanged by the colleges. In later centuries a priest could use a liturgy phrased in a tongue which he did not understand, and the people took part in rites whose meaning was only dimly apprehended, yet which meant something. Processions and holidays, amusements and sacrifices impressed the state worship upon the popular mind. We shall see later how the full flood of Greek and Oriental religious ideas broke upon Rome and how myth and story were adopted to furnish the picturesqueness which the native religion lacked. For, especially in the fourth and third centuries B.C., new cults were brought into the religious practice of the state, though as regards myth and ritual they were stamped with the Roman mark. But the influx of ideas never penetrated to the heart of the old Roman religion, which was fixed in its essential nature. It continued both in the city and in the countryside, as is abundantly clear when the evidence of literature and inscriptions becomes most plentiful. Educated men of the last century B.C., conversant with Greek philosophy and criticism, might regard it as mere form; but those same men held offices in the sacred colleges and encouraged its practice in the state, and indeed too in the family. Augustus, the first Emperor, was not building on nothing when he sought to rescue from the collapse of the state, and to re-erect, the old Roman religion and the morality associated with it.

A strong morality was supported by this cold and formless religion, and the growth of morality was unhampered by mythology. For the Greeks Homer had enshrined stories of gods in everlasting verse – till in a later age critics had protested that his gods were less moral than men. The

Romans had no sacred writings beyond the formulae of prayer; there was therefore no myth-made morality to be undone. The individual's business was to establish right relations with the gods, not to speculate about their nature. The city's business was the same, and the individual was left to indulge in private beliefs of his own if he wished. The Roman attitude is always the same – tolerance, provided that no harm was done to public morals and that no attack was made upon the state as a state. The Roman attached to the god his own morality as he developed. The process may be illustrated thus:

One of the earliest powers to be individualized was the power of the sunlight and sky; it was called Jupiter, if indeed Jupiter was not the single spirit from which other *numina* were individualized. It was an early custom to swear an oath in the open air under the sky, where no secret could be hidden from an all-seeing power. Under this aspect of an oath-witnessing power Hercules received the epithet *Fidius*, 'concerned with good faith'. Again the individualising tendency came into play; *Fides*, 'good faith', was personified, the abstract from the epithet. The process went on; epithets were attached to *Fides* to denote the different spheres in which *Fides* operated.

This ability to abstract an essential characteristic is part of the mental process of the lawyer. The Romans showed the capacity to isolate the important and to pursue its applications; hence their jurisprudence. In the kind of speculation which demands a creative imagination but seems almost to ignore the data of experience they failed. But, more important, the isolation of moral ideas gave those ideas an added emphasis; in the household and in the state moral ideas received a status similar in kind to the status of the 'powers' themselves. They were real things in themselves, and were not created by opinion; they had objective validity. It is beside the mark to suggest that abstract qualities can scarcely have inspired any warmth of religious feeling, for neither did the 'powers' themselves. Moreover, the qualities soon found embodiment in a long line of 'noble Romans'. The point is that moral ideas were enveloped with the sanctity of religious cult, and later literature is not understood if the virtues, to which appeal is so often made by historian and orator, are not interpreted in this way. They were bound up with the duty laid upon household and state to worship the gods. Here is to be found the root of that sense of duty which marked the Roman at his best; it often made him unexciting, but he could become a martyr for an ideal. He did not argue about what was honourable or just; his notions were traditional and instinctive and they were held with an almost religious tenacity.

> *The man of firm and righteous will,*
> *No rabble clamorous for the wrong,*
> *No tyrant's brow, whose frown may kill,*
> *Can shake the strength that makes him strong.*

Thus, the Roman was hard.

Perhaps the conception which shows best the Roman point of view is that of the '*Genius*'. The idea of the genius begins from the *paterfamilias* who in begetting children becomes the head of a family. His essential character is isolated and given a separate spirit-existence; he carries on the family which owes to him its continuance and looks to him for protection. Thus, as a member in that mysterious sequence son–father–son–father, the individual gains a new significance; he is set against a background which, instead of being a continuous surface, is broken up, and the pieces are shaped, and one of them is shaped like himself. His genius, therefore, is that which puts him in a special relationship to his family which went before him, and has perished, and to his family which is yet to be born of his sons. A chain of mysterious power links the family from generation to generation; it is because of his genius that he, a man of flesh and blood, can be a link in that unseen chain.

Here we may recall the custom, indeed the right, by which noble families set up in a recess of the central hall of their houses, at first, wax-masks and, later, busts of their ancestors who had deserved well of their family or of the state. In the most solemn domestic rites of the household these busts were made to associate. There was no question of ancestor-worship or appeasement of the departed; rather, it was a demonstration that they and all for which they stood still lived on and that they supplied the spiritual life to the family.

It is but a slight development of the genius to attribute to each man who is potentially a *paterfamilias* a genius and to each woman a Juno; for this there was Greek precedent. But the original idea of '*Genius*' was capable of expansion. Just as the genius of a family expressed the unity and continuity underlying successive generations, so genius was later made to belong to a group of men unrelated by blood but joined by common interests and purposes through successive stages. The group acquires an entity of its own; the whole is more than its parts, and that mysterious extra is the genius. Thus in the early Empire we hear of the genius of a legion; the officer of today will readily agree that the 'traditions of the regiment' feebly expresses what he feels; genius is more personal. So, too, we find the genius of a town, of a club, of a trading community. We hear of the genius of branches of the civil service – the mint and the customs, for example; it is natural to compare our own 'high traditions and ideals of the service'. The Romans had an amazing power of envisaging the personality of a 'corporation'; they were sensitive, we should say, to the spirit behind it, and that is what they said quite literally when they spoke of a genius. And it is not surprising that in Roman law the law of 'corporations' was carried to a high degree of elaboration.

The power which has guided in the present will guide in the future, and so the genius of Rome comes close to a 'Providence' protecting her, and to a mission which she is fulfilling.

It is clear that in the household of the farmer the wife occupies a position of authority and responsibility. Among the Romans, theoretically she was under the guardianship of her husband, and in law enjoyed no right. But she was not kept in seclusion, as in a Greek household; she shared her husband's life and set a standard of wifely and mother-ly virtues envied in a later age. Parental authority was strict, not to say severe; and parents received the respect of their children, whom they took round with them in the several occupations on the land or in the village or in the house. Education was given by the parents, and was 'prac-tical'; even the stories of the past were so framed as to point a moral, and the Twelve Tables of Law were learnt by heart.

Later ages looked back to the primitive simplicity of early times, and no doubt idealized it. But it was not myth; in the third and second century B.C. there was literature which testified to it, for men then wrote who had come in contact with men who had been thus brought up. The 'old ways' survived as realities, and still more as ideals. If we enumerate some of the virtues which Romans regarded as characteristically Roman throughout their history, we must connect them with the native endowment, the pur-suits and manner of life, the early struggles for survival, and the religion of the first centuries of the Republic. They will be seen to be all of a piece.

First in every catalogue of virtues comes some recognition that a man should admit his subordination to something external which has a 'binding-power' upon him, and the term for this, *religio*, has a wide application. For a 'religious man' the phrase is usually 'a man of the highest *pietas*', and *pietas* is part of that subordination of which we have spoken. You are *pius* to the gods if you admit their claims : you are *pius* to your parents and elders, and children and friends, and country and benefactors, and all that excites, or should excite, your regard and perhaps affection, if you admit their claims on you, and discharge your duty accordingly ; the claims exist because the relationships are sacred. The demands of *pietas* and of *officium* (duty and services, as in 'tender offices') constituted in themselves a massive and unwritten code of feeling and behaviour which was outside the law, and was so powerful as to modify in practice the harsh rules of private law, which were only a last resort.

Gravitas means 'a sense of the importance of the matters in hand', a sense of responsibility and earnestness. It is a term to apply at all levels – to a statesman or a general as he shows appreciation of his responsibilities, to a citizen as he casts his vote with consciousness of its importance, to a friend who gives his advice based on his experience and on regard for your welfare; Propertius uses it when assuring his mistress of 'the seriousness of his intentions'. It is the opposite of *levitas*, a quality the Romans despised, which means trifling when you should be serious, flippancy, instability. *Gravitas* is often joined with *constantia*, firmness of purpose, or with *firmitas*, tenacity; it may be seasoned with *comitas*, which means the relief given to over-seriousness by ease of manner, good humour, and humour. *Disciplina* is the training which provides steadiness of character; *industria* is hard work; *virtus* is manliness and energy; *clementia* the willingness to forgo one's rights; *frugalitas*, simple tastes.

These are some of the qualities which Romans most admired. They are moral qualities; they may even be dull and unexciting. There is nothing among them to suggest that intellectual power, or imaginativeness, or sense of beauty, or versatility, or charm – that hard-worked word nowadays – appealed to them as a high ideal. The qualities which served the Roman in his early struggles with Nature and with neighbours remained for him the virtues above all others. To them he owed it that his city-state had risen superior to the older civilization which surrounded it – a civilization which appeared to him to be limp and nerveless unless stiffened by the very virtues which he himself had painfully cultivated. Perhaps they can be summed up under *severitas*, which means being stern with oneself.

The manner of life and the qualities of character here described make up the *mores maiorum*, the manners of one's ancestors, which are among the most potent forces in Roman history. In the broadest sense the phrase may include the political constitution and the legal framework of the state, though generally such words as *instituta*, institutions, and *leges*, laws, are added. In the narrower sense the phrase means the outlook on life, the moral qualities, together with the unwritten rules and precedents of duty and behaviour, which combined to form a massive tradition of principle and usage. To this tradition appeal was made when revolutionaries laid violent hand on political practice, on religious custom, or on standards of morality or taste. The constancy of this appeal, made by orator and poet, soldier and statesman, showed that it had not lost its force even in the most troubled times or in the latest ages. Reformers might ignore tradition, but they could not deride it; and no Roman dreamed of destroying what was old merely because it was old. From the end of the Second Punic War, beneath the reverence for the noble Romans who embodied this noble tradition, a new note begins to be heard – the note of regret at the passing of something of value which is too remote from the present corrupt age to be restored. It begins in Ennius, 239–169 B.C., who has been described as the Chaucer of Roman poetry, 'Rome stands built upon the ancient ways of life and upon her men'. Cicero, whose appeal to the *mores maiorum* is incessant and sincere, receives from Brutus the compliment that for 'his virtues he could be compared with any of the ancients'. No higher praise can be given to a woman than to describe her as 'of the old standards of life', *antiqui moris*. Horace, whose affectionate tribute to his father is genuine, says of his own upbringing,

> 'Wise men,' he'd add, 'the reasons will explain
> Why you should follow this, from that refrain:
> For me, if I can train you in the ways
> Trod by the worthy folks of earlier days,
> And, while you need direction, keep your name
> And life unspotted, I've attained my aim:
> When riper years have seasoned brain and limb,
> You'll drop your corks and like a Triton swim.'

The tradition lived, at least as an ideal, to the last days of the Empire.

Looking back, we cannot say that a religion such as the old Roman religion was likely to promote greatly the religious development of man; it carried no intellectual appeal and was, therefore, unable to contribute a theology. But it is certain that with the associations and habits which clustered round it its contribution to Roman character was very great; by it, too, a mould was fashioned in which later ages tended to cast the new and formless mixture of ideas which reached them from the older Mediterranean cultures. Great men were almost canonized for their characters or for their achievements. To the beliefs and manners of those days we must ascribe that sense of subordination or obedience to exterior power, whether a god, or a standard, or an ideal, which in one form or another marked the Roman to the end. To the same source must be traced the feeling for continuity which, while assimilating the new, preserved the type and refused to break with the past; for the future could be faced with greater security if the value of the past were conserved. The early practice of rite accompanied by formal invocations and crystallized into a 'sacred law' helped to develop that genius in law which is Rome's great legacy; and the law of the state borrowed a reflected sanctity from its sacred counterpart. Law presupposed obedience and was not disappointed. The position of the head of the family, the respect given to the mother, the training given to the children, were confirmed and strengthened. The validity of moral ideas was securely established, and ties of natural affection and of service to friends and dependants were made firm by a code of behaviour which lay outside legal obligation and was of compelling power. The formal nature of religious observance preserved Roman religion from the gross manifestations of Oriental ecstasy, even if it forbade warmth of personal feeling; and the attitude of toleration towards religion which marked the republican and imperial ages originated, paradoxically, with a people who assigned the utmost importance to state religion.

The result of the religious, moral, and political tradition of Rome was a stability of character which eventually assured the stability of the Roman world; and it should not pass unnoticed that a people, whose nature it was to look backwards, itself moved forward and placed progress within the power of others.

CHAPTER II

We have gone far enough, perhaps too far, without a framework of history to guide us. What follows for the next few pages is a rough guide composed of three unequal parts. First is a very brief account of the periods into which Roman history is generally divided; second comes a rapid glance at the expansion of Rome in the Mediterranean so that in later pages we may know what we mean by Rome at any given time. Third is a brief summary of the development of the government of Rome; it can give no indication of the rich political experience of the Romans, but it should not be skipped, however jejune it may be.

(a) KINGS, REPUBLIC, EMPIRE

We shall tell our story clearly if we treat first what was done first, if we keep the temporal order of events.

UNKNOWN AUTHOR OF *Ad Herennium*

Roman history is usually divided into three parts, though other divisions would have some justification: the period (i) of the Kings, (ii) of the Republic, (iii) of the Empire.

(i) According to the commonest tradition, Rome was founded in 753 B.C., and Tarquinius Superbus, the last of the kings, was ejected in 510 B.C. The accounts of this period as they have reached us are largely legend, but legend which enshrines elements of history: these elements have been isolated, with the aid of archaeology and the comparative study of origins and the method of 'survivals'. This period concerns us hardly at all.

(ii) The period of the Republic, 509 B.C. to 27 B.C., is the period in which Rome won her position in Italy and then in the Mediterranean, in which she gained, in success and defeat, her political and administrative experience and learned from the civilization of other peoples. The last century (from 133 B.C.) is one of political disorder, commercial and financial expansion, and moral confusion. Here arise new problems of central and provincial government, of defence, of economics and land distribution, of military leaders backed by armies and defying the state, of the rise of powerful business interests, of new ideas in philosophy and religion, and new modes of conduct. Here are the names which everyone knows, the Gracchi, Sulla, Pompey, Crassus, Julius Caesar, Brutus, Antony, Cicero, and the rest. Our evidence for this period is fuller than for the earlier centuries.

(iii) The third period, beginning in 27 B.C., is the 'Empire' or, better, Imperial Rome. This title needs explanation. The greater part of Rome's Empire in the territorial sense was acquired in the second period; as a description of the third period 'Empire' refers to the method of government, namely by an Emperor. But Augustus, whose power controlled the Roman world from 27 B.C. to A.D. 14, insisted, and insisted sincerely, that he had restored the 'republic', and he wished to be known as *Princeps*, or leading citizen : hence the phrase 'Principate' is often used to denote the earlier part of the Empire, and the 'reigns' of individual 'Emperors'. Thus, the division 'Republic' and 'Empire' is very largely of our labelling, and it is misleading.

The first two centuries of this period are, speaking generally, the constructive years of the Empire, the years in which the Romans began to leave their most permanent impress on the nations of the Roman world. They close with the age of the Antonine Emperors, A.D. 138–193, of which Mommsen, the great German historian, said, 'If an angel of the Lord should be minded to compare the territory ruled by Severus Antoninus as it was then and as it is now and to decide in which of the two periods it was ruled with the greater intelligence and humanity, and whether, in general, morals and happiness have improved or deteriorated since those days, it is very doubtful whether the judgement would be in favour of the present day.' Our own Gibbon had already said much the same.

Then came a century of confusion, till in A.D. 306 Constantine became Emperor, and Byzantium, renamed Constantinople, and now Istanbul, became in A.D. 330 the capital of the eastern half of the Empire, whence arose the East Roman Empire, heir alike of the Greek and of the Roman tradition.

(b) FROM THE SEVEN HILLS TO
THE ROMAN ORB

... to sing a hymn to the gods with whom the Seven Hills have found favour.

O all-nurturing Sun, that with thy chariot of fire bringest forth the day and hidest it again and art born anew other and yet the same, may it never be thine to behold aught greater than this city, Rome.

HORACE

Thou hast turned into one city what was formerly the orb of the world. RUTILIUS CLAUDIUS NAMATIANUS

Italy is a mountainous peninsula, with the 'backbone' of the Apennines lying nearer to the eastern than to the western coast and often reaching to the sea itself. The harbours lie on the west and south. From Alps to 'instep' is about as far as from John o' Groats to the Isle of Wight, nearly 600 miles. The angle of the peninsula is such that the heel is 300 miles further east than is the north-east coast at Ravenna. From the heel to Greece is some 50

miles, and from the west corner of Sicily to Africa only
100 miles.

If the mountains of Italy, with their upland valleys,
rich in corn and oil and wine and always beloved of the
Romans, have caught the love of centuries, there are also
three plains which have played no small part in history.
In the north is the wide plain of the valley of the river Po
(*Padus*) which rises in the Western Alps south-west of
Turin (*Augustus Taurinorum*) and so cuts across the
peninsula. When the Romans first reached this plain they
found it occupied by Gallic tribes, and it was always
known to them as Gallia Cisalpina, Gaul on this side of
the Alps. In the middle of the west coast is the plain of
Latium; through its northern end runs the second largest
river of Italy, the Tiber, which rises in the Apennines due
north; light vessels could travel up its lower reaches. The
third plain is the Campanian, further south on the west
coast; Neapolis (Naples) and Cumae were famous cities of
Greek foundation in ancient times; Vesuvius has been its
threat through the centuries.

We begin with the second of these plains. We must
omit all the attempts made by archaeologists to trace the
descent of the 'Italic' tribes from beyond the Alps, and we
start with the Alban Hills, south-east of the Latin plain
and the mouth of the Tiber. Here, at Alba Longa, was
built the first city of the Latins, founded, as legend said, by
Ascanius, son of Aeneas of Troy, whence the Romans
derived their alleged Trojan ancestry; Romulus and
Remus were his descendants. Here was the sanctuary of
the god of the surrounding villages, Jupiter of Latium.
Clearly we must imagine a 'gathering together' of villages
drawn closer by common needs of defence and worship
and trade; and no doubt Alba Longa was typical.

Later, these same hill-men moved down to the plains

and settled upon the site of the 'Seven Hills' of Rome. They were a pastoral folk. Their earliest festivals were concerned with the interests of shepherds; milk, not wine, is the earliest offering, and wealth was reckoned in cattle; the very word for 'money', *pecunia* (whence 'pecuniary'), means 'head of cattle'. They found other men of kindred race, Sabellian and Sabine, moving upon the plain and settling upon the higher ground; from the fusion of these settlements Rome took her origin. From her central position her soldiers could move north and east and south – along the valley north and east, and down the plain to the south; they soon learned the value of 'interior lines'. Indeed, some have thought that the site of Rome was chosen from the first as an outpost against the Etruscans to the north. And here, for the moment, we leave the Romans, as they join with outlying settlements, and turn to agricultural pursuits and trade with Etruscan and Greek merchants.

To the north of the Tiber lay the Etruscan empire. The Etruscans were probably sea-wanderers (from the East?) settled at last in Etruria, or Tuscany – cruel, overbearing, worshipping gloomy gods of the underworld and divining the future from the study of the organs of slaughtered animals. They built enormously solid walls to defend their cities, and they traded with Greek cities and with Carthage in Africa, and thus 'borrowed' from civilizations superior to their own. From the sea they penetrated into the Campanian plain, and in the seventh century tried to move south to occupy it, circling round the hills to the east to avoid the swamps, and seizing some of the Latin towns on the high ground.

About the time of the Latin migration to the 'Seven Hills', Greeks began their long process of seizing the best harbours on the south and west coasts of Italy and the

eastern side of Sicily; the Carthaginians, too, occupied
the western half of the island. At first the Greeks wanted
only trading stations, but in time colonies were sent from
Greece to establish cities which soon became among the
fairest of the Mediterranean. Perhaps the earliest Greek
settlement was Cumae, on the bay of Naples, in the eighth
century, and of great moment to Europe; for from the
Greeks of Cumae the Latins learned the alphabet; the
Etruscans too adapted the same letters to their purpose,
and passed them on to the inland tribes. From Cumae,
also, Italy may first have learned of Greek gods, such as
Heracles and Apollo. But the chief settlements of the
Greeks were in the extreme south of Italy and in Sicily.
Syracuse and Agrigentum in Sicily, and Tarentum,
Sybaris, Croton, and Rhegium in South Italy are all Greek
in origin. They are most important in Roman history, for
through them Rome came into full contact with the
Mediterranean world.

The Etruscans and the Greeks were the two most powerful influences during Rome's early years. The rest of Italy
was sparsely inhabited by tribes, many akin to the Latins.
They lived in comparative isolation in their hills, tending
flocks and tilling the land and grouping together into
settlements, as geography allowed, for defence and trade
and worship.

Now let us return to the Romans. The first three kings
were Latins, the last three were Etruscan. The last of these
was ejected by violence (traditionally 510 B.C.), and the
word 'king' became anathema to the Romans. Yet the
Etruscan influence remained. Temples and rites survived;
Jupiter was still enthroned on the Capitoline Hill, Diana
on the Aventine. The insignia of Etruscan rulers became
those of Roman magistrates, the 'ivory chair', the bundles
of rods with two axes bound up with them (*fasces*). But,

more important, Rome acquired an organization which was to turn her into an imperial power.

Till about 270 B.C. Rome fought perpetually for existence in Italy, and her fight could not cease till she was recognized as a leading power. The highest qualities of courage and resourcefulness were called for; one tribe after another was overcome, and was incorporated on varying terms into the Roman state or sphere of influence. Leagues and alliances were created. At one crisis – the sacking of Rome by roving Gauls in 390 B.C. – the Latin cities failed to aid her; they suggested federation, and Rome made up her mind that safety lay only in their conquest. At great self-sacrifice she reduced them to obedience, and then went forward as tribe after tribe appealed to her for aid, and eventually for alliance and the extension of her 'rights' to their cities. At last Thurii, in the 'instep', appealed for aid against Tarentum. Rome hesitated – and agreed. Tarentum brought in Pyrrhus, King of Epirus across the Adriatic; and Rome emerged from his invasion of Italy the leader of the Greek states in South Italy. Thus, she passed into the sphere of the Carthaginians whose trade covered the seas of Sicily and the Western Mediterranean. After half a century of struggle (264–202 B.C.) it was decided that Rome should become a 'world power', and that the lands of the West should be ruled by an Aryan, not a Semitic race.

Before the Punic wars are summarized (for the Carthaginians were Phoenicians, in Latin *Poeni*, whence *Punicus*), two observations must be made. Though Rome seems to be ceaselessly at war, she was at war because of the force of events and the logic of her own temperament. Round her were powers older, more experienced; some were ambitious, and their neighbours were afraid : threats to Rome's allies were threats to her, and, speaking generally, she went to war to remove those threats. After the struggle with Carthage she found herself drawn against her will into further commitments. Later she became attracted by conquest, for a new type of Roman was growing up to whom the East offered tempting opportunities. Secondly, the resolute determination not to take the easy path of temporary but inconclusive appeasement resided in the people as a whole, inspired and led by a deliberative assembly, the Senate, which controlled policy, yet strictly had only advisory powers. In this period the Senate rose to its highest point of political and moral ascendancy; towards the close its influence diminished, for its nature was profoundly affected by the enlarged horizons of empire.

The power with which Rome was now to close in a struggle for the destinies of the Western Mediterranean was Phoenician in origin. Unlike other Phoenician settlements, Carthage had become a land-power, for she overran vast tracts as far as Gibraltar and turned them into the farms of her wealthy land-owners. Her sea-power had secured a small empire in Sicily and Sardinia and South Spain. The Romans feared her dominance in the seas west of Italy, and they had now come face to face with her in Sicily. Already they were allied to Carthage and to Syracuse; and when they had to choose between them, they chose Syracuse. After many bitter defeats at sea, Regulus landed with a Roman army in Africa and was defeated and taken prisoner; eventually a sea-battle was won, and the Carthaginian general Hamilcar was forced to withdraw from Sicily. Hostilities ceased. The war taught valuable lessons to both sides. The Romans tested the loyalty of their Italian allies and learned much about naval warfare. The Carthaginians found that mercenaries were no match for legionaries, and set to work to train

Spanish troops; but they never cured the government's incessant suspicion of its own generals in the field or the threatened disloyalty of its African subjects.

Before the war broke out again, Rome annexed Sardinia and Corsica for safety's sake, and so created the first 'provinces'; Sicily soon followed. Thus were laid the foundations of the Roman provincial system. Raids by Gallic tribes were repulsed, and the Po valley became a subject land. Rome was becoming the leader of Italy.

Meantime, the insight and energy of Hamilcar had extended Carthaginian control of Spain; and when Massilia (Marseille), an old ally of Rome, was threatened the signal was given for the Second Punic War.

The story of this great struggle cannot be told here. Hannibal crossed the Pyrenees, the Rhône, the Alps, and descended upon Italy, where for fourteen years his army lived upon the Italian countryside, attempting with little success to detach the Italian allies from their loyalty. After initial failures Rome dared not risk open battle. Q. Fabius Maximus, called 'the Delayer' for his 'Fabian' tactics, might nibble at the invading army, but no conclusion followed. Roman nerves stood delay no longer. A general was appointed and charged to put an end to the invader. At Cannae in 216 B.C. the Roman army was annihilated – and Rome never rose to such heights. Patiently she set to work to regain lost ground, and Hannibal was provoked to advance on the city. Three miles away he turned aside; for no ally joined him, no army met him, no proposals of peace were sent to him. He withdrew. His brother Hasdrubal hastening into Italy from Spain was defeated and slain; and at Rome P. Cornelius Scipio urged and was allowed to undertake the invasion of Africa. At Zama in 202 B.C. victory was won; Carthage was broken.

There are many interesting features about this war.

Rome might have expected it to be fought in Africa or
Spain; it was fought in Italy, and it fused Italy into a
whole. Rome might have expected some respite after
victory; she was committed to years of severe fighting in
Spain to prevent Carthaginian consolidation there; and,
if Spain was divided into two 'provinces' in 197 B.C., much
work still lay ahead. She might have expected that after
the wars in Spain Carthage would give no further trouble;
but Carthage attacked Numidia. Rome decided upon
extreme measures; yielding to the incessant demand of
M. Porcius Cato that 'Carthage must be destroyed', she
destroyed the city in 146 B.C., and Africa became a Roman
province. Finally, Rome might have expected the thanks
of posterity and some measure of admiration for her inflexible courage and endurance through sixty-five years of
war and threat of war. But such prosaic virtues are apt to
pale beside the romantic figures of Dido and Hannibal;
and neither Regulus, made immortal in an ode of Horace,
nor Scipio Africanus can restore the balance in English
minds. When Vergil, the poet of the Augustan age, told in
the *Aeneid* the story of Aeneas' journey from the still-
smoking Troy to found a new Troy on the Seven Hills, he
made his hero halt on the shore of Africa where Carthage
was being built by Dido, her queen. Aeneas stayed as her
guest and lover till his duty to the Trojan gods drove him
once more in search of the promised land. Betrayed and
deserted, the queen killed herself, and the moving scenes
in which Vergil presents the whole drama enlist modern
sympathy on the side of the Carthaginian queen; Aeneas
the reader of today can scarcely understand. The curse of
deadly enmity between the two nations called down by
Dido was extinguished only by the extinction of Carthage
herself.

Hannibal makes a different appeal. As a boy he swore

on the altar of Moloch undying hatred of Rome. His crossing of the Alps, his long and patient harrassing of Italy, his approach to Rome and his turning aside, his readiness to restore order in a defeated Carthage and his refusal to take kingly power, and finally his last desperate fling at his old enemies as the tireless counsellor of Rome's enemies, his suicide – here is all the material for a heroic figure overshadowing the less attractive Roman, who nevertheless survived to achieve for the world what no other achieved.

To return to the sketch of Roman Imperial expansion. In the West we shall hear of no further undertakings till 125 B.C. In the East the story is very different, and for its understanding it is necessary to glance back at the empire of Alexander the Great.

Alexander died in 323 B.C., and his empire fell into fragments : the largest units remaining intact were Macedon, Syria, and Egypt. To Macedon belonged Greece; to Syria belonged Babylonia and Assyria; to Egypt, Phoenicia, and the Greek islands; Pontus and Pergamum, in Asia Minor, and India reasserted their independence. All these kingdoms possessed in varying degree a mixture of Greek and Oriental culture. The coast of Asia Minor had long been occupied by Greeks, who had adopted something of Oriental thought and habit; from the cities of Greece the less cultivated Macedonians had learned a higher civilization, while Alexandria in Egypt was cosmopolitan, and became the centre of new scientific, literary, and philosophical studies. Over the whole of this world a culture was spread which goes by the name of Hellenistic. It was not moribund, for it put out new growths and endured in many aspects for another thousand years. But it lacked spontaneity and vigour; it was sophisticated and self-conscious, apathetic and disillusioned. Yet no sooner is this said than elements of originality in it occur to the mind. But politically at least it was rotten; for it contained either monarchies of the Oriental pattern, with an absolute ruler revered as divine, a court of ambitious nobles and laxity of standards, or else quarrelsome city-states, living on their past history and unable to control themselves or their dependencies, or loose confederacies perpetually in a state of coalescence or disruption. With this state of affairs Rome was now coming into contact. In the East she found a civilization already long established; in the West she brought to Italians, Spaniards, Gauls, Africans, and countless others a civilization higher than their own. Hence her conduct in East and West differed markedly.

Often most reluctantly, sometimes not unwillingly, now from self-interest, now from loyalty to allies and genuine impulse to liberate cities enshrining the culture which she was beginning to admire, Rome committed her armies to ever further Eastern campaigns. She aided one state after another; she promoted alliances; she ringed round her advancing interests with ever-widening circles of buffer states pledged to commit no breach of the peace; she experimented with the balance of power. But her efforts called for qualities in the East which were not forthcoming; and by 146 B.C. she had been compelled, in the interests of good order and peaceful trade, to occupy Macedonia (in 167) and Greece (in 146). In Asia Minor she relied on establishing protectorates of allied states stretching as far as the boundaries of Armenia and the river Euphrates. Egypt, too, which had been saved by the intervention of Rome, acknowledged her supremacy. Thus no direct government was exercised by Rome further east than the Aegean, and she had little cause in later years to regret her tolerance. But, even when she acted firmly and set up provinces in the East, the civilization and language which she found there she left untouched to last for centuries longer.

Firm action was to come in 64–62 B.C. In 88–84 B.C. Mithridates, King of Pontus, in concert with Tigranes, King of Armenia, overran most of Asia Minor and slaughtered thousands of Roman traders; the Pontic fleet dominated the Aegean, and forces were landed and welcomed at Athens. The Greek cities throughout Greece threw in their lot with the invader, and the whole of Greece appeared to be lost. But Sulla defeated the Pontic armies in 86 and 85 B.C., cleared Greece, and in the following year a Roman fleet under Lucullus dominated the Hellespont. Ten years later Mithridates again set the East ablaze. The campaigns of Lucullus carried him very far east. But matters did not go well for the Romans on the sea, for piracy flourished throughout the Mediterranean and Roman fleets were embarrassed for lack of regular supplies. Therefore, in 67 B.C., Pompey was appointed with extraordinary powers; he suppressed piracy in an organized sweep starting from Gibraltar, and he invaded Pontus and Armenia. He invested Jerusalem, and for the first time Roman power made contact with the Jewish people; thus began that troublesome problem. Pompey then 'settled' the East; boundaries and governments, finance and commercial relations were re-ordered. The province of Cilicia was enlarged, and Bithynia, Pontus, Syria, and Crete all became provinces; Cappadocia, Armenia, and many minor states were left as independent kingdoms. The appointment of Pompey to that command, it should be noted, was the step which led to the fall of the Republic.

It is time now to return to the West. Here we must pass over wars in Spain and Africa and the suppression of a slave revolt in Italy, and concentrate on four main features: first, the safety of the western end of the Alps; secondly, the relationship between Italy and Rome; thirdly, the conquests and provincial policy of Julius Caesar; and fourthly, the problem of the eastern end of the Alpine frontier.

The Alps might appear to be a natural protection of impassable strength. Actually Hannibal, and later his brother, had surmounted them. In the land to the north and east great migrations of people had been going on for some time; they were hard pressed towards the west by other peoples in search of land. In 113 B.C. a large host of Germans, accompanied by other tribes who had been caught up by them, appeared at the eastern end of the Alps. They had already defeated one Roman army in Illyria. They pushed their way westwards without turning aside into Italy; and there was momentary relief. But in 109 B.C. they appeared in Southern Gaul, which thirteen years before Rome had annexed and turned into a province. They carried all before them, defeating two armies at Arausio (Orange). In three years Marius trained the first professional Roman Army, re-equipped and led it to defeat the most menacing of the tribes in Northern Italy and in Gaul. The hordes passed further west, and a hideous danger was over.

In 91 B.C. a danger no less serious threatened the City of Rome. The Italian allies rose in open revolt. For two centuries they had borne the burdens and hazards of war; they now desired the very incorporation in the citizen body which earlier they had rejected in favour of alliance. For, as we shall see, Roman citizenship was an increasingly valuable possession. Yet, as it increased in value, Rome granted it the more sparingly, the citizens of the capital jealously guarded its extension, and for years Italian

resentment smouldered. Their rebellious manifesto proclaimed a new capital, called Italica, at Corfinium, and
the proposed constitution was modelled closely upon the
political traditions which its would-be citizens were at the
moment rejecting. Justification of Rome could go no
further, though that does not forgive her shortsightedness
in refusing citizenship. In a swift and resolute campaign
the rebellion was broken by Sulla, and a series of laws
granted enfranchisement to all Italians. Italy ceased to be
a confederacy. The city-state had had its day, and a new
idea was born. How it developed and what were its implications must be seen on a later page.

The third feature is the conquest of Gaul and its
organization by Julius Caesar during the strenuous nine
years 58–49 B.C.; his own account of his work is, of course,
the famous *Caesar's Gallic War*. When he entered Gaul,
his governorship covered a very small Gallic province:
when he left Gaul, the province covered France and
Belgium and he had 'shown the way' to Britain. Italy's
frontier of the Western Alps was now secure.

But, fourthly, the eastern end yet remained to be closed,
and it was not till Tiberius, who later became Emperor,
had undertaken long years of fighting on the Rhine
and lower Danube that this quarter was secure; the
province of Raetia (Eastern Switzerland and the Tyrol),
Noricum (Austria), and Pannonia (Carinthia and
Western Hungary) eventually formed the north-eastern
bulwark.

Now comes the great turning-point in Roman provincial policy. Augustus had intended to draw the frontier
at the Elbe, and so to include in the Empire the German
tribes who menaced Gaul and to shorten the northern
frontier. But in A.D. 9 a Roman army of three legions was
cut to pieces by Arminius (Hermann) in the depths of the

Teutoberg Forest near Osnabrück: the XVII, XVIII, XIX
legions never again appeared in the army list. In the
papers which Augustus left at his death he advised no
further extension of the Empire.

Yet the Empire was enlarged when necessity counselled
it. To protect the Balkan peninsula the tracts south of the
lower Danube became in A.D. 46 the provinces of Thrace
(Southern Bulgaria, Turkey, and the Greek coast at the
head of the Aegean sea) and of Moesia (Serbia, Northern
Bulgaria, and the Dobruja). The province of Britain was
also added. In A.D. 107 Trajan created the province of
Dacia (Rumania) as a bulwark to protect Moesia and
added others in the East which his successor surrendered.
Thus by the end of the second century the line of the
'Roman Circle' was drawn – Rhine, Danube, Asia Minor,
Syria, Palestine, Egypt, Africa, Spain, France, Britain –
and Rome had 43 provinces to administer. In A.D. 270
Dacia was evacuated, and Diocletian (A.D. 284–305) re-
organized the whole Empire, including Italy, into 120
administrative districts.

In the history of Rome's imperial expansion self-
defence must be accounted the first motive; but trade
inevitably followed and the first motive was mingled with
that of commercial exploitation; and in the second century B.C. reasons of safety were sometimes alleged in order
to hide greed and ambition. The first two centuries A.D.
were the age of assimilation, and thereafter self-defence
was again to the fore as the most urgent consideration.
Rome never fought to impose a political idea or a religious
creed; with unique generosity she left local institutions
and manners of thought and life untouched. She fought to
'impose the ways of peace', and by peace she meant the
positive blessings of settled order and security of life and
property with all that those blessings imply.

(c) FROM CITY-STATE TO REPUBLIC IN RUINS

Cato used to say that our state excelled all others in its constitution; in them, for the most part, an individual had established his own form of state by his laws and institutions ...; our state, on the contrary, was the result not of one man's genius but of many men's, not of one man's life but of several centuries and periods. Genius had never been so profound as to enable any man at any time to overlook nothing; nor, if all genius were concentrated in one man, could he have such foresight as to embrace everything at any one moment; actual experience stretching over the ages is needed.   CICERO

It is due to our own moral failure and not to any accident of chance that, while retaining the name, we have lost the reality of a republic.
CICERO

The sketch just given has described the growth of Rome's foreign power. We now turn to the government of the city, of Italy and the provinces, touching on social matters only in so far as they cannot be avoided. We shall catch a glimpse of the process by which the constitution developed and of the ways in which it was modified by the needs of governing overseas possessions. We shall see the tentative methods by which Rome first governed her possessions, and the failure of those methods; we shall then discover why the constitution which she laboriously wrought broke down and how it was replaced. In other words, we are concerned with the process by which Rome turned from a city-state into an Empire. In the story of this process certain elements will for the most part run through from the beginning of the Republic to its collapse. These elements are, for example, the Senate, the people, the magistracy, and its later development the pro-magistracy. Roughly, the magistrates of various kinds and ranks are the executive; the pro-magistrates are ex-magistrates appointed for special posts outside Rome, as for example, governors of provinces or specially appointed generals of armies. Roman constitutional history is largely the slow change in the duties and powers and functions of these elements, and in the relationship between them. If Polybius was right in saying that the Roman constitution rested on a balance of power, the balance was maintained at different periods in different ways. Finally, the crash came. And, when the Empire replaces the Republic, we shall find the same elements furnishing most of the material from which the edifice will be built. The Romans preferred to tolerate apparent anomalies and even absurdities, to rely on good sense and understanding and restraint, to observe the spirit instead of the letter, and to keep tried and familiar institutions. They preferred to do this rather than to press matters to logical and unworkable conclusions or to define closely in written articles of a constitution what was best decided by compromise, or to set up new institutions born of the impulse of the moment. They were happiest in adapting to new uses something already wrapped round with tradition and sentiment and practice.

As a clue to the account which follows it might perhaps be useful to mark out in rough-and-ready fashion the following phases. First, up to the Punic wars the potentially autocratic powers of the magistrates were gradually reduced by the opposition of the 'people' on the one hand and the Senate on the other; further, the 'people', or the plebeian families, asserted itself in opposition to the Senate, or the patrician families. In the second phase, that of the Punic wars, the Senate was supreme in fact, though not by right, and its supremacy was justified; the magistracy was superior to the pro-magistracy. In the third phase, the pro-magistracy was the strongest power; the Senate was almost impotent through lack of constitutional authority, the people attempted to reassert itself with justification in theory. But its opportunity was lost and its very nature had changed; moreover, new factors were introduced – an influential business class and a new aristocracy more jealous of the privileges which it had once attacked than the old aristocracy ever was. In the fourth phase, the first *Princeps* (or Emperor) learnt the lessons of three centuries of Roman constitutional history and built from the debris of the fallen Republic a structure of government which lasted for two centuries at least as a government still Roman in essentials.

We have referred already to some kind of 'gathering together' or 'dwelling together' of little settlements of various tribes to form the city of Rome. How it was brought about and what were the causes and the contributions from the composing elements no one can say. Tradition and reasonable deduction from survivals suggest that this primitive association was loosely held together by common interests symbolically expressed in common 'rites' of religion, 'communion in sacred things', *communio sacrorum*. The community was ruled by a king, who was a patriarchal ruler, the elected officer or magistrate and the priest of the whole people. One of his most important duties was 'to take the auspices'; briefly, this means making sure that things were right between the gods and the community. Apparently, a new king was appointed by the heads of the leading families (*patres*); the 'sacred things' were transferred to him by the *patres* in whose keeping they were, and the choice was confirmed by the community as a whole. The king held supreme power (*imperium*), appointed officials, dispensed justice, led in war, and ordered religious worship.

The Senate was the council of the heads of leading families; they were members for life and with them reposed in times of transition the 'sacred things'. They offered advice to the king only when consulted; they proposed a new king, but could not appoint him unless the whole people approved.

The people as a whole gathered only when summoned to hear pronouncements from the king, to take part in religious rites and to witness certain acts, as, for example, disposal of property by will, which later fell under the head of private law. All our information about these early times is very vague. Equally obscure are the changes brought about by the Etruscan supremacy in Rome. We hear of a new organization of the whole people on military lines, with the landholders and wealthier citizens serving in the front ranks since they could afford to arm themselves. But the autocratic rule of the Etruscan kings brought about the ejection of the alien dynasty, and the title 'king' was for ever accursed.

The power of the king passed to two magistrates originally called 'praetor-consuls' (that is, 'leaders' who are 'colleagues') and in time merely 'consuls'; in times of crisis supreme power was entrusted, though in fact very rarely, to a 'dictator', who held it for a limited period and for a specified purpose, the magistrates continuing in their own spheres on sufferance. And so with the creation of consuls begins that curious principle of 'collegiality' which runs through the history of the Roman magistracy – the principle of colleagues in office who have the power of vetoing each others' proposals; positive action therefore depends upon colleagues acting in concert. The change, however, made no break in the chain; the consuls 'took the omens' and held their power (*imperium*) in direct succession from Romulus. The consuls held office for one year; they were appointed by the whole people in assembly, from whom they received their *imperium*, and the choice was ratified by the Senate. The position of the Senate remained the same. But in all probability their number was soon enlarged by the inclusion of new heads of families; and it is clear that annual tenure of office by consuls and the collegiate nature of their office tended to give the Senate increased influence; for it was permanent, while the magistrates changed.

The history of the next two centuries is the history of conflict and manoeuvre for position. Soon after the expulsion of the last king, there broke out into open conflagration a discontent which had long smouldered. The struggle is known, rather misleadingly, as the struggle of the 'orders'. As we have seen, it is impossible to know the composition of the Roman community in early times. But it is at least clear that among the component elements there were families of substance – land, flocks, and buildings – with tradition and claims to eminence in past history both as leaders in war and as bearers of its burdens. Such families had their roots in the land; their men were farmers and soldiers; they were known as 'patrician'. But there were others; some were attached to the leading families and dependent on them; others were landholders and traders and craftsmen, for under the Etruscan rule Rome had developed as a commercial centre, doing business by sea and land. There were also fugitives from surrounding settlements, and members of neighbouring tribes, attracted by commerce or drifting in as the result of the confusion wrought by wars. These were 'plebeians', but all were citizens and members of the assembly; there was no question of a distinction between conquered and conquerors, franchised and disfranchised. What drove a line between them was custom. Thus, by the working of the constitution, patrician magistrates nominated patrician successors for acceptance by the assembly, and the measures submitted by patrician magistrates had to be ratified by the *patres*. Discontent soon showed itself. The plebeians took to holding meetings in a 'Council of the Plebs' which was informal and outside the constitution. The main grievance was the unfettered power of the consuls. The ensuing struggle can be sketched only in essentials, but it is important to see that the plebeians were concerned not with attack in order to obtain privileges but with defending themselves. A promise was made that no Roman citizen should be put to death inside the city without appeal to the people; on active service discipline might demand otherwise. Delay brought about a threat by the plebeians, partly carried out, to found a rival city. This move won from the patricians, who needed man-power for the army, a concession of tremendous importance. Plebeians should have annual magistrates of their own, called 'tribunes of the people', at first two, later ten. They were to be elected by the 'Council of the Plebs', i.e. by plebeians only. But the tribune, like the Council, was at first strictly outside the constitution; he was given not *imperium* but a special limited power (*potestas*) to aid plebeians against individual acts of a patrician magistrate; his person was inviolate; he convened the 'Council' and invited it to pass resolutions. Later, as we shall see, the tribuneship acquired far-reaching powers of veto in the whole field of government; and still later the tribunician power was an essential component of the power of the Emperors.

Next came a demand to curtail the consul's power by law. It was countered by a promise to draw up and publish a code of law. This is the celebrated Twelve Tables, which probably went no further than expressing publicly what was existing usage. But it was an event of tremendous significance in the history of law and of Europe.

Now opens further struggle in which the tribunes exchanged the passive role of 'protector' for active efforts to change the constitution; for Rome was growing, and the plebeian element became more important. The most powerful lever for effecting change was created when, in 449 B.C., the tribunes obtained that resolutions of their own Council of plebeians (that is to say, part of the state, though the major part) should bind the whole state (under certain conditions unknown to us); the first 'plebiscite' to be passed ensured the permanent institution of the tribunate as part of the state machinery. Soon, marriages between the 'orders' were recognized.

The next demand was for a 'plebeian' consul. The patricians countered by suggesting that the consulship should be put in abeyance and six 'consular tribunes' with consular powers should be appointed from either order. The 'consulship' was saved, but for fifty years out of the next seventy-eight (i.e. to 366 B.C.) the plebeians succeeded in insisting on consular tribunes; and entrance to the office of *quaestor*, an assistant to the consul, was won for them. The patricians again countered by creating the office of *censor*; undoubtedly the task of taking the census was becoming more important with the increase of population and of land acquired by war; but no doubt the patricians also hoped to reduce the powers of the consulship before they had to yield it to the plebeians.

The rest of the story can be briefly told. Between 367 and 287 B.C. the plebeians won the following concessions: one consulship must be held by a plebeian; the 'sacred college' of priesthoods was thrown open; the plebiscites required no ratification by the *patres*. The struggle was over, for the Council of the Plebs was now in theory the 'sovereign' power. The patrician families remained; but if they still exercised power it was by prestige and moral influence and not by law. The plebeians were now the preponderant element in the state, in both numbers and wealth. For the future, power theoretically lay with them.

The tribunate remained, though it was now unnecessary, for its original purpose had been served. But it was used to new and sinister purposes a hundred and fifty years later as a weapon in a new struggle between a new governing class, largely plebeian, and a new and less worthy populace.

In 287 B.C. it seemed that all was ready for rule by the people. But it was not to be. The Punic wars now broke upon Rome; energy was necessarily deflected in directions other than political change. Whether, if there had been a prolonged period of peace, the Senate would have been denied its coming supremacy is doubtful; for it was in a strong position and its leadership was powerful. But in any case two hundred years of war came, and the experience and wisdom and steadfastness necessary for the surmounting of times of strain and danger lay with the Senate. Its moral supremacy produced its supremacy in the whole conduct of affairs.

For by the time of the First Punic War its nature and composition had changed since the early days of the Republic. The task of appointing to the Senate lay with the consuls, as succeeding the king; the 'collegiate' principle secured some measure of responsible choice. Later the task was transferred to the censor; for it was clearly sensible that the consul should not appoint the man whom, as a senator, he was later to consult. Soon, by custom which hardened into a right, all ex-magistrates – and there were by now several grades of elected magistrates below that of consul – passed into the Senate, and so by the avenue of the magistracy plebeians passed into its ranks. The Senate, therefore, was largely a body of men who had been elected to various magistracies by the people, with whom they naturally kept in touch as they stood for office after office; when their public service was over, they entered the deliberative assembly to place their experience at the disposal of the state. Thus the prospect of a permanent seat in the Senate was opened out to the successful candidate to annual office; and office became a means as well as an end, and was therefore valued in rather a different way than before, though the consulship was always an honour coveted for its own sake. Thus there arose a new rank or status, or, if the term is understood to have nothing to do with birth, a new nobility – of office. Patrician birth was now only a matter of private pride; the new 'nobility' carried public esteem and was proud, often with the exclusiveness of the newly promoted, of its responsibilities and position. Meantime, the magistracy became more closely attached to the Senate, for the magistrate would one day take his place among senators; he therefore consulted it with a new deference.

The exigencies of war pointed to the Senate as the only directive power. The people was assembled with difficulty, the Senate was at hand and was manageable in size. Continuity of policy and swift decisions had to be made; treaties had to be drawn up and supplies granted, often in a hurry. Experienced soldiers and statesmen, with knowledge of 'foreign parts', were in its ranks. And so one precedent after another was established; the 'opinion of the Senate' now became 'the decree of the Senate': as a body it ceased merely to discuss the problem submitted by the magistrate and now initiated discussion, and so it gathered into its hands practically all state business. Its conduct of affairs during the hardest years of war was in general excellent; if later it fell from its high standard of efficiency and moral integrity, it was for reasons which we have presently to consider.

Rome acquired her supremacy in Italy partly by war, partly by taking full advantage of the disunity of the various tribes and attaching them one by one to herself in a loose confederation. By every means in her power she secured that they should look to her for help and advantage rather than to each other. Her near neighbours were incorporated as citizens into her body politic; to others she extended a limited citizenship which conferred rights of trade, together with enforcement of those rights at law, and freedom of inter-marriage with Roman citizens. Others were bound by various treaties of alliance, carrying duties and privileges but also independence to conduct internal affairs.

At a few points in Italy colonies of Roman citizens were planted to guard coasts and roads: they were offshoots of Rome. Elsewhere 'municipalities', i.e. the original towns, were granted full franchise: both these communities had a generous degree of self-government. Appeal against local magistrates could be taken to Rome. Prefects were sent out to try cases in both towns and country districts; they represented the praetor at Rome, who was the chief judicial magistrate.

But, when the lands beyond Italy were annexed, different measures were called for. At first, Rome was, in general, reluctant to 'create' a 'province'; she was content at first to disarm and tax, as e.g. Macedonia in 167 B.C. 'Province' implied annexation and annexation implied a Roman governor. But after 146 B.C. she did not hesitate. Sardinia and Sicily had been placed after their conquest under a praetor. But the praetors were needed at home. Therefore, after 146 B.C., a new device was adopted, for which there was precedent. The *imperium* of consuls had often been prolonged to deal with a military emergency, and the holders of the command were then said to act

pro consule, on behalf of the existing consul. From 146
B.C. pro-consuls and pro-praetors were invested with full
imperium and sent out to govern the provinces. They were
required to govern within the 'charter of the province', a
charter drawn up by a senatorial commission which defined the status of the various communities, fixed
boundaries and rates of taxation and methods of local
government, and sanctioned the use of local law. The
charters were drawn up in a generous spirit, partly because Rome did not want the burden of over-detailed
administration, partly because she was at heart generous.
All depended on the governor's observance and interpretation of the provisions of the charter and on his sense of
honour; for his opportunities for misgovernment and self-
aggrandizement were vast, and he was with difficulty
brought to book.

Now let us go back to Rome and sketch in the barest
outline the main features of the period of revolution, the
last 100 years or so of the Republic (to 31 B.C.).

The challenge to the constitution was made thirteen
years after the destruction of Carthage in 146 B.C. It came
from the tribunate, then held by Tiberius Gracchus.
Measures to cure the depopulation of the countryside and
to arrest the decline of agriculture – both of them evils
due to war – were his programme. But for success he
needed more than one year, and he must perforce nullify
the veto of his colleagues in the tribunate whom the
Senate had brought over to its side. Both needs could not
be satisfied without a breach of usage. He deposed his
colleagues, and thereby gave his enemies the chance of
denouncing him as the usurper of autocratic power. He
fell a victim to the very violence to which, so it was afterwards maintained, he had first appealed. The lesson of
his fate was noted by men who came after him, for he

had raised the question 'where lay the sovereignty?' and
had perished. So perished, too, nine years later, his
brother Caius, who, beginning with an attempt to widen
the Senate by importing new blood, ended by proposing
to give some of its powers to the new class of influential
business men and conciliating the populace of Rome by
selling corn at a low price. He sought, too, to bring
before a court other than the Senate, governors who mis-
governed the provinces. For two years he was tribune,
and he took his proposals straight to the people whom at
first he dominated as by a spell; but he too was killed.
Here was another lesson: the people could be roused, and
when roused might for the moment achieve their purpose;
but the tribunate, with no military power behind it, was
useless to maintain those achievements against resistance.

The age that follows is the age of great individuals
seeking so to alter the machine of government as to adapt
it to the new stresses, yet patiently preserving, as far as
they could, the old component parts. But impatience frequently prevailed, and impatience was fanned to white
heat by the personal rivalries which followed upon the
competitive claims to adjust the government to satisfy
ambition or the claims of faithful armies. For amid the
fierce passions loyalty to the state, as it was understood in
the old days, was forgotten; long-service and triumphant
armies were now loyal to their general, who in turn was
loyal to the claims of his army for pensions, which meant
land. The needs of the state were of secondary importance; indeed, its only salvation lay in the precarious align-
ment of the loyalty of armies to generals and of generals
to state. And, as the government did not deserve loyalty
and generals had rival generals to consider, such align-
ment seldom occurred.

The change in the attitude of the army was brought

about largely by Marius' creation of a professional long-service army, trained and equipped on new lines, to meet the menace of the German tribes beyond the Alps. Henceforth, the army, recruited from the Mediterranean, looked to its general; gone for ever was the old Italian army, composed largely of citizens. The new army was a mighty weapon at all times, but in its early history it was from the state's point of view double-edged; it was not till the time of Augustus that the right method of handling it was found.

Sulla used it for two purposes; first, to defeat the threat of foreign enemies and the menace of the Italian allies; secondly, to enforce upon Rome what it had never had before, namely a written constitution and the legal recognition of the supremacy of the Senate. He then stepped into retirement to watch his constitution work. But it was not now the same kind of Senate that had justified its unofficial rule during the Punic wars. It was now inefficient and self-seeking, intent upon filling its pockets by the exploitation of the provinces. The constitutional changes were soon abolished, though much of Sulla's judicial and administrative machinery remained, as it deserved.

In 62 B.C. Pompey returned from the East where he had wielded the power specially entrusted to him by the Roman populace. He needed nothing but the ratification of his acts, if his work of organization there was to be put on a lasting basis; he had foolishly (by the standard of the time) disbanded his army. It was not until Julius Caesar came to his aid and laid pressure upon the government that his work was ratified. But Caesar demanded his reward; Pompey was to see to it that he was given a prolonged command in Gaul, so that the consolidation of the frontier, begun by Marius himself, could go ahead. For nine years Julius Caesar stayed on this frontier; France and Belgium were added to the Empire, and the first steps in their civilization were taken. It was the work of a military commander and his army, not of the people and Senate of Rome. Who, then, was entitled to the controlling hand in government? Caesar answered the question in his own favour, as had Sulla before him; but Sulla could rely only on the support of the few, and Pompey had declined to take the opportunity, though the lesson of the command entrusted to him was clear. It was Caesar who realized that, though he might have to fight, he could win if he could gain the sympathy of the majority by his programme of intentions.

While he was in Gaul the Senate had watched his growing power with alarm, and ceaseless manoeuvres had been exercised to rob him of power. His agents, tribunes loyal to him, his friends, and all those who owed or looked to him for wealth or advancement defeated these manoeuvres. But towards the end the Senate had won over Pompey, who now liked to take up the role of their champion, and had placed an army under his control. Caesar saw the point, and with his army crossed the river Rubicon in the north of Italy, and by that act declared civil war.

In an incredibly short time he scattered the Pompeian army, pursued part of it to Spain, and defeated the rest in 48 B.C. His 'clemency' astounded the world.

For four years Caesar controlled the state, and in 44 B.C. he was murdered because he was setting himself as 'king' over the Republic. So Caius Gracchus had been murdered some ninety years before. Of his legislation we must here say nothing, except that he showed his understanding of the need of a new policy towards the provinces, and of widening the basis of government at home and of the economic organization of Italy. But he evolved no new constitution, no theory to justify his own power or to provide for his successor; and above all he did little to win the imaginative sympathy of his time. His great-nephew and adopted son, Octavianus, later known as Augustus, had forty-five years of rule.

The political, social, and economic problems in this last century are of great interest, and the evidence for part of them includes that fascinating study, the Letters of Cicero. The chief problem, as is clear, is the weakness of the central government to control the provincial governors, who were in the provinces to execute the wishes of the government at home. We have seen that the principle of shared power, or collegiality, weakened the magistrates, i.e. the executive, in relation to the legislature. Now the provincial governor had *imperium*, i.e. the same kind of power as the consuls at home, but he was alone with no colleague; the only controls therefore were (a) annual office, (b) his neighbour with equal power in an adjoining province, though this latter might be rather a provocation than a check. But the check of the short span of office was removed by the people itself, who voted long terms to one general after another, exalted them into great com-manders-in-chief, demanded their services as popular heroes on all occasions, and weakened the only control yet left, namely laws against misgovernment and prosecu-tion to enforce such laws. These were of little avail amid the strife of parties and the people's clamour in support of its favourites, and the greed and ambition of the governors themselves. Here is to be found the cause of the fall of the Republic. Not till the Empire was it discovered (a) how to secure loyal governors, (b) that the true Roman policy to-wards the provinces themselves was not exploitation but local self-government in a Roman loyalty. Other prob-lems are of great interest, particularly the agrarian question – the condition of agriculture, the depopulation of the country and the drift to the towns – and especially to Rome, where an idle rabble demanded even greater doles – the question of the reinstatement of the veterans, the failure of the soldier to make a farmer, and the dearth of land. This last question touched keenly the Italian 'allies', and led to the 'Allies' War' (see p. 40): for the Italian cared little about voting, but he cared much about the fear of dispossession to make place for a time-expired soldier. Only Roman citizenship could save him, and he fought and won. Finally, there was the rapid growth of wealth and the equally rapid decay of old standards in public and private conduct; and political life knew a corruption from which it had been free.

The twelve years which followed saw the world divided into parts organized one against the other by rival generals and rival parties. The strife, which cost thousands of the best lives of the time and left the West exhausted, was ended by the battle of Actium in 31 B.C., when Octavianus finally defeated Marcus Antonius and Cleopatra. At last came the era of peace and order for which the people had yearned for centuries. We shall see later, first, why the battle of Actium was one of the great turning-points in history; secondly, what use Octavianus, whom we shall hereafter call Augustus, made of his long reign.

CHAPTER III

(a) THE NEW WAYS AND THE OLD

What remains of the old ways in which Ennius said that the Roman state stood rooted?
CICERO

How did it come about that the old Roman ways ceased to maintain their hold?

The new ways were, of course, due to the influence of Greek habits of thought and life; and it is important that by 'Greek' we should understand not the supreme expression of the Hellenic genius as given in four or five of the great authors of the fifth and fourth centuries B.C., but the culture which was spread over the Eastern Mediterranean, and which itself looked back to the great age of Athens for most of its inspiration. In many respects it had seized upon the least important aspects because it was incapable of living up to any great moment; it had debased Greek language, Greek literature, and Greek character. The Greek masterpieces were available for reading and were read by many; but the Greek men whom the Romans now began to meet in daily life were not always as the fifth-century Athenians. Though the Romans employed the artistic and professional skill of the 'Greekling', on the whole they despised him for his character; and they despised him the more because he had not lived up to his former greatness.

In considering the relation of one culture to another, we cannot avoid metaphors, dangerous as they are. 'Influence', of course, means 'flowing in'; but the new ideas were deliberately imported by Roman minds attracted to

them! We sometimes speak of a man 'assimilating' the
ideas of another; and strictly this should mean that he
takes into himself alien ideas and turns them into something not quite the same and builds them into the fabric
of himself, choosing what he will receive or appropriating
unconsciously, and embodying into himself only what his
nature is capable of converting into his own tissue. The
process of conversion may take time; at first, the mass of
imported ideas may remain 'crude', and *crudus* in Latin
means 'undigested'; but eventually – to change the
metaphor – the alien ideas are woven into the texture together with the native original element, and the finished
fabric is a new creation. For some of Greek thought the
Romans had little use, as, for example, metaphysical
speculation; some they appropriated in part, as, for
example, the practical bearing of mathematics, but not its
theoretical foundations; a great deal they put through
their robust and matter-of-fact minds, modified, and
handed on in a shape which was adapted for everyday use
by the peoples whom they governed. It is important,
therefore, to be on guard when using in this connexion
such terms as 'borrowing' or 'appropriating' or 'taking
over', and to beware of condemning the 'borrower' for
'borrowing'. Not to have 'borrowed' would have deserved
the more censure; deliberately to incur and readily to
admit the debt in itself implies some sensitivity and appreciation and honesty. 'Borrowing' may be a quite false
description, for one idea starts another and it is hard to
say where the credit lies. Finally, it is of greater service
to posterity to 'borrow' and to convert to use as much
as a limited capacity can so convert than vainly to
attempt to annex an alien whole without discrimination,
and so to ensure its certain and total decay. In spite of
Roman solidity – or stolidity – of character, the Greek

genius left its mark; in spite of Greek 'influence' the Roman spirit preserved its individuality, its genius; Greco-Roman civilization thus became the root of European civilization.

The old and the new points of view are perhaps best seen in particular men. P. Cornelius Scipio, surnamed Africanus, may be taken as exemplifying the new type of Roman, Marcus Porcius Cato as embodying the old type, and Scipio Aemilianus, who was adopted from the Aemilian family by the son of Scipio Africanus, as the forerunner of many who attempted to reconcile the old and the new ways.

The Cornelian family had already given men of note to the service of the state. When at a time of crisis in the Second Punic War the assembly of the people looked for a bold leader capable of ending the intolerable strain, and, when men of experience hesitated in face of the awful hazards, Scipio Africanus, aged twenty-four, confidently offered himself. He was given the task and he succeeded. His whole life was of a piece with that act. From that time he dramatized himself; he loved the spectacular and invested himself with a religious aura as though he were the favourite of divine will. In Spain he was dazzlingly successful; his magnanimity attached the tribes to him; they offered him the crown, for they said he was god-like, and when he refused they furnished him with troops. In Africa he won over by sheer charm kings who were neighbours of Carthage, and Rome wondered whether such familiarity with foreign potentates was altogether right. Story made him stay as Hasdrubal's guest, or discuss with the exiled Hannibal the relative merits of each other in comparison with Alexander. At home he brushed aside custom and law, standing for offices before he was qualified by age, and receiving encouragement from an admiring people. He affected the grand manner and studied every action; even at the end, when in semi-exile he lay dying, he 'refused his body to an ungrateful country'. Hitherto the great men of Rome had been such as Cincinnatus, who left his plough to serve the state in time of crisis, and returned to it when his work was done. In Scipio the Roman people were offered a new kind of hero – a hero who asserted individuality in defiance of tradition, who based leadership on power of personality, and made a romantic appeal to the imagination now awakening in the ordinary Roman. How did such a type of hero arise?

It arose – if we continue to illustrate 'movements' and 'influences' by men – when Livius Andronicus, a Greek slave captured at Tarentum, composed as a reading-book for his master's children a metrical Latin version of Homer's *Odyssey*. The work passed beyond its original intention; here was a new literature; stories of heroes who were at once godlike and human. No longer the statuesque forbidding heroes of early Rome, slaves of duty, but warm-blooded and erring and lively and full of zest. And what leaders of men, swaying multitudes by their word and guiding by their wise counsel the future of city and army! After Homer, Greek comedies were translated and were combined with native Italian farces and burlesques, and Roman comedy arose. Moreover, once the heroes of Homer – Agamemnon, Odysseus, and the rest – had been treated, there was no reason why Roman subjects should not be chosen, and Naevius, of Campania, wrote an epic of the First Punic War, combining Greek and Italian legend and motif. Ennius followed with an epic in hexameters which included the Second Punic War; the *Iliad* was his model, but his own strong Roman character shines through; and in his tragedies, though they owe much to the Greek tragedian Euripides, the moralizing and philosophical discussion is Roman. And the achievements of Alexander and the legends clustering round his name made their appeal to the imagination of men like Scipio and stimulated them to dreams of similar exploits.

The rise of this literature and the performances of tragedies and comedies brought before the Roman public new types of human character, isolating the individual and drawing attention to special features. The opportunities for men of strong character to influence the life of society and of the state were revealed to the intelligent; the new knowledge of Greek legend and history showed that it had been done; there was no reason why it should not be done in Rome, and arguments could be drawn from Greek philosophy to justify it. The new ideas of Greek thought spread with the Greek language, and a lively and imaginative mind like the mind of Scipio Africanus grasped their implications and created for itself a role as a Roman leader of a new type.

M. Porcius Cato was born in 234 B.C. and was brought up on his father's Sabine farm, which he inherited. At the age of twenty he distinguished himself fighting under Q. Fabius Maximus against Hannibal, and served to the end of the war. At the age of thirty he was quaestor to Scipio in Sicily, and was with him in Africa; in 198 B.C. he was praetor of Sardinia, three years later he was consul, and in 184 B.C. he was censor. He was soldier, lawyer, statesman, farmer, writer, but above all a 'character'.

As a young farmer he took up the cause of his neighbours in local law-courts, for he was a good speaker ready to champion the right. A friend advised him, in spite of his plebeian birth, to seek a larger sphere for his energy and gifts in Rome itself, whither he went. Till the day of his death at the age of eighty-five he was engaged in ceaseless labour, laying about him in law-court or senate-house or published work with the same lusty vigour and ruthless courage with which he had engaged in combat on the battle-fields; of this conflict his fame and his body alike bore many scars. At home his life was of the simplest, for he trained himself in austerity; as a general he remained the soldier of the ranks, marching on foot and carrying his own arms. As a provincial administrator, he was inexorable and was proud of it; he cut down expenses in the interest of the governed, and scrutinized every item charged to the home government, 'which under his administration never seemed more terrible nor yet more mild'. He beat down contracts for public works, and raised them for the farming of taxes. Once he suspected an enemy or a friend of dishonourable conduct, he 'never shrank from a quarrel on behalf of the commonwealth'. His speeches were famous; Cicero, who had read over a hundred and fifty of them, says 'they show all the qualities of great oratory'. Their pungent aphorisms became proverbial; their skill was a model, for he knew all the tricks. His son he educated himself, composing for him text-books of grammar, law, and history; for he would not let him owe 'so great a thing as his learning' to anyone else. He taught him to ride and box and fight and swim and farm. No doubt he was an exacting father; but 'a man who beat his wife or child', he thought, 'laid hands on what was most sacred', and a good husband he thought 'worthy of more praise than a great senator' – his highest praise. As censor he carried one ordinance after another to check, by high taxation or sheer prohibition, the luxury encouraged by the flow of wealth into Rome. His influence was amazing; his counsel was sought on all things, for, says Livy, though he was so 'all-round', you would have

thought him born to do the very thing to which he was
laying his hand. Not even old age broke his vigour of
mind and body; towards the end of his course he showed
the same ardour 'with which many approach the beginning, when their fame is yet to make': though he had
achieved fame, he did not relinquish his labours.

This was the man who fought Hellenistic influence in
Rome, and naturally lost – though a name which becomes
a rallying cry for centuries has not altogether lost. It is
easy to caricature Cato, for he lends himself to it; and
there are many traits in his character which repel us. His
treatment of his slaves was inhuman; he gloried in his
asceticism; he seemed to deny pleasure to others and
therein to gain his own twisted pleasure. He may be called
narrow, uncompromising, insensitive, vain, sancti-
monious; ostentatiously priggish, if it were not for his
humour; self-righteous, if he were not fighting for an
ideal. He may have cast himself for a part, and overacted,
but his sincerity remains. It is also easy to misinterpret his
opposition to the fashionable cult of things Greek; there is
something to be said on his side. He knew Greek all his
public life, for Greek was necessary to any statesman who
had dealings with the East. He knew well the works of
Greek orators and historians; he took a Greek translation
of a Carthaginian work as his model in his book on agriculture. He tells his son to look at Greek literature, but
not to lay it to heart, for they are 'a scoundrel and in-
corrigible race'. It is not intellect which Cato despises, but
the contemporary use of intellect to undermine character.
His ideal is the citizen of high moral principle, based on
tradition, realizing himself in the commonwealth and its
business, and so creating a triumphant government pre-
eminent for enlightened policy and massive integrity. The
Greeks whom he came across were politically dead; yet

they came to Rome and talked and talked. When Carneades and Diogenes, philosophers both, were in Rome, they made a great stir by their lectures, 'it was like a great wind sounding round about the city': and Cato was afraid. For in his view Greek oratory had nothing to say, and many words with which to say it: his own definition of an orator was *vir bonus dicendi peritus*, a man of high character who can make a good speech. The sophists of Socrates' day had boasted their skill to make the worse appear the better cause, and the Greeks of the third and second centuries were their heirs. The self-assertion of individual personality, such as Scipio loved, was the reverse of Cato's ideal – action, in the midst of a community, inspired by a moral motive: personal influence and charm were dangerous, thought Cato, and went to the other extreme. The modern self-culture led to self-indulgence in the name of art and learning and fashion. The springs of action as discovered by 'the noblest Romans' were dried up at their source; for Cato all true knowledge issued in action, and action revealed the man. Introspective absorption in self and its culture meant the collapse of a common morality; and then would emerge the 'leader', casting his spell by cleverness of word and promise over a characterless people.

It is possible that the best statement of Cato's motives is given by a Greek who lived a hundred and fifty years before him, namely Aristotle. In that mine of political wisdom, the *Politics*, he says that the greatest contribution to the stability of a constitution is made by 'education' or training for the constitution, though 'nowadays everyone despises it' (and Aristotle had witnessed the decline of the city-state). Laws, he says, are of no use unless the members of a state are trained and educated in the constitution. But such training is training not with a view to actions which will please the government, oligarchy or democracy, but with a view to actions on which oligarchy or democracy will be able to base their own particular constitutions. Young oligarchs should not be trained to luxury, nor democrats to the belief that freedom is doing what you please. 'A man should not think it slavery to live according to the constitution; he should think of it rather as his salvation.'

The Roman constitution *was* an oligarchy and it was based on law and custom: the sons of the oligarchy *were* multiplying their luxuries: the cult of the individual's tastes and caprices in indifference to all else was being interpreted as freedom: the laws and the unwritten codes were becoming of less use. Cato trained himself and wanted others to train themselves, and the best school was the Roman school.

When Scipio was publicly charged with malversation of public funds in his campaigns, he invited the people to go with him there and then to the temples to render thanks for his victories; for it was the anniversary of the battle of Zama. He was triumphant – on personal influence and popular sentimentalism. No wonder Cato was afraid.

Scipio was eventually found guilty, but none dared arrest him, and he died in semi-exile. Cato survived him; but, as he himself said, it is not easy to have to render an account of your life to an age other than the age in which you have lived.

Cato could not win; the Roman city-state was passing away. The wealth of the world, and Asiatic notions of the use of wealth, were entering Rome.

The ideal of Scipio Africanus and the ideal of Cato stood in open contrast. When Cato was an old man and Scipio already dead, an attempt at a reconciliation of the two ideals was made by Scipio Aemilianus, son of Aemilius Paulus and adopted into the family of his uncle, Scipio Africanus. At first Aemilius Paulus himself undertook the education of his sons, and, as they grew older he procured for them Greek teachers, grammarians, philosophers, and painters. When Scipio grew up, he ranked as the most cultured man of his day; he and his friend Laelius gathered round them poets, philosophers, artists, and historians, giving them more than encouragement: for Scipio and Laelius both wrote and were sympathetic and constructive critics. Plautus had already written, round Greek plots, comedies full of boisterous farce strikingly Roman in character: now Terentius Afer (known today as Terence) wrote comedies of character, smooth and correct in language, full of psychological study and moral musings and destined to exercise great influence on European comedy. They failed to attract the populace, who preferred 'tight-rope walkers and gladiators' and left the theatre empty. But they made a profound impression in educated circles, and not least because the Latin language was being moulded to new uses. Thus Terence, an African slave-boy transported to Rome, a student of Greek comedy and of Roman character and a genius in the use of the Latin tongue, became the friend of the leading citizen of the day. So did Polybius, the Greek captive, who was freed and took up his abode in Rome, and travelled about with Scipio on his campaigns; he wrote from the detached Greek point of view the history of Rome, and a most valuable and judicious history it is.

Now Scipio combined with his love of Greek literature and art a Roman simplicity and an admiration for old ideals which won the highest praise from Cato himself – 'he alone has wisdom, the rest are empty shadows,' – a line from Homer. Like Cato, Scipio was censor and sought to check the growth of luxury both by law and by example. He was anxious to prevent further expansion of the Empire; he imposed discipline upon the army; he refused to court the Roman populace whom he frequently angered, and he boldly maintained that Tiberius Gracchus had been rightly slain. 'So perish all who do the like again' – another Homeric line. Scipio in his turn was murdered, says Cicero, by his political enemies, in 129 B.C.

Here, then, was an attempt to combine new ideas and old principles. It failed, as it was bound to fail, before the seductions of wealth and power. Noble families fell from their honourable traditions; the new populace of Rome and the great cities within the Empire exerted their growing strength to secure ends that were no less selfish than those of the governing class and probably not as enlightened. But the antithesis of the Roman spirit and the surrounding culture continued; there were to be many Catos and many Scipios of both types, though of less heroic stature, in Roman history. In spite of everything, the Roman spirit broke through all that threatened to submerge it.

(b) CICERO

The race of men shall perish from the earth before the glory of Cicero shall perish from their memories.   VELLEIUS PATERCULUS

Cicero stands near the end of the age of conflict and disruption. From his pages we can reconstruct much of the story of his time, as seen from the viewpoint of a member of the aristocracy. He was born in 106 B.C. and was put to death by Antony a year after the murder of Julius Caesar in 44 B.C. His extant works take up eighteen volumes in a small pocket edition published in 1823: three volumes of 'rhetorical' treatises (or literary criticism and 'education'), six volumes of speeches written to be delivered in Senate or law-court, four of letters, four of philosophical works, and one of fragments. In all these pages there is little that tells us of the manner of life led by the majority; in Latin literature, as in Greek, the outlook is that of the few. In Rome the government was in the hands of an oligarchy drawn from families ennobled by service to the state and counting among its members the most highly cultivated men of the day. In the writings of Cicero the strength and the weaknesses, the blind selfishness, the massive culture, and the corruption of public and private integrity stand out clearly. He was a 'new man', that is, he did not belong to one of the old families; he came from Arpinum, and like many before him he had migrated to Rome to stand for office as the preliminary to a public career. He was eminently successful, and after his famous consulship in 63 B.C. had held a short and inconspicuous term of office as proconsul in Cilicia. In senatorial circles – for, of course, he was a senator – he moved freely, for he was a leading advocate, politician, and man of letters. Occasionally a slight trace of social uneasiness can be detected. He loved Rome and was miserable when away from it. To him and to his circle the only work which counted as work was in the service of the state (*negotium*); all else, no matter how urgent or exacting, was 'time off', even though it might include a man's main livelihood. For this class land was the only worthy occupation; trade and industry were not acceptable pursuits. It was not that these men were above money; money was their curse and some of the largest fortunes of history were gathered into the hands of men like Lucullus and Crassus, and were often expended on luxuries wicked and futile; moreover, towards the end of the Republic senators evaded the rules forbidding them to have interests in trade and industry and transacted business of all kinds through intermediaries. What they disliked was retail trade and the routine of manufacture. But they were on close terms with contractors and producers 'in a big way' and with financiers and bankers; and they readily sold their estates and country houses and bought others, and speculated in the land and 'house-property' markets.

These men of senatorial rank moved about Rome and Italy and the provinces as though they were a race apart. Their pride in Rome was intense; their appreciation of themselves could scarcely fall far behind. To them Rome was the capital of the world, and they knew it, as others did not. They had started their careers with military service, and they had held offices in Rome and had then gone out to govern provinces. Royal houses had received them, men of letters and distinction had conversed with them; councils and assemblies had decreed them honours and privileges, even offering to them the religious veneration accorded to their own kings and heroes. The tide of war had fallen back before them and before the majesty of Rome, and their power of organization had brought order out of chaos. The might and the prestige of Rome were due to their forefathers who had flung an empire from west to east and north to south, and they were the guardians. That they were sometimes disloyal to the highest traditions and often enriched themselves unscrupulously was true enough. Their heads were turned not so much by power as by wealth. All the same, many did realize the weighty obligations of the *Imperium Romanum*, and they realized them with Roman *gravitas*. They *were* a race apart, for, even if they had not found the right method, they were in fact conscious of doing a work for which they were set apart. Had not three hundred and six men from the Fabian family perished in the service of the state in 477 B.C., and had not the fortunes of the family hung upon one young boy? Other families could show comparable records.

Below this 'order' was the order of the 'knights' (*equites*). In the early days of Rome, when the duty of military service carried with it the duty of providing arms and accoutrements appropriate to wealth, the citizens were classified according to property. Those with a particular assessment were required to bring a horse with them to war and to join a cavalry squadron – in fact, to become a knight. This title survived long after recruitment was on another basis, and it denoted eventually men who possessed a property qualification of 400,000 sesterces (about £12,000 today). By Cicero's time the 'knights' were a powerful class; they were free from the inhibitions about business which hampered the senator and free from some of his sense of honour; their interests were in state contracts, in the commercial expansion or development or exploitation of the provinces. Cicero's great friend Atticus, with whom he corresponded for many years (the letters are still extant), was a knight, and he was a cultivated man of literary and philosophical interests, rich and unostentatious, who had far more leisure time on his hands than Cicero or members of the Senate. Since about 130 B.C. equestrian influence in the state and in politics had grown enormously; knights were a recognized 'order' with certain privileges and duties and prestige. To the knights the traditional aspects of Roman power probably appealed little; they were interested in stability, and the first Emperor relied on the order very greatly when he built up his new 'imperial civil service'.

At Rome the rest of the total population of perhaps three-quarters of a million was made up of shop-keepers, artisans and 'small men' pursuing a great number of occupations, together with many thousands who were always in a state of semi-idleness because there was nothing urgent. A great proportion was of foreign birth, for Rome attracted men and women from all countries; and freed slaves swelled the populace. These freedmen were a growing class whose influence was increasing. There were also the slaves. Rome harboured all nationalities, and more were yet to come within the next century; but already by the time of Cicero there were very many – Greeks and Syrians and Egyptians and Jews and Germans and Africans. Of course, not all these had the citizenship.

These were the classes – Senate, knights, people – whom it was Cicero's ambition to unite in order to promote some kind of social stability after a century of strife. He realized that in all quarters of the state there were men who were 'sound at heart'; he felt that, if they could be brought together, they could create a healthy public opinion which would be proof against irresponsible revolutionaries on the one side and the 'leadership' of one man which could develop into autocracy. He called his ideal the 'united front' of sound elements, the *concordia ordinum*. He realized, as some of his writings show, the need of some kind of leadership, but his difficulty was to find the right name and the right role and still more to imagine himself the right man. His last philosophical work was the *De officiis*, written after the murder of Caesar – a work which for centuries was read by every educated man in Europe and now is scarcely read at all. It contains Cicero's last musings upon life and politics and human behaviour, and it is crammed full of a wisdom embodying a political experience such as no Greek had ever passed through; its influence on European thought has been profound. It probably cost its author his life, for it made clear that he thoroughly approved of the murder of Caesar, and Antony could not afford to leave him alive.

But Cicero's efforts were doomed to failure; in 63 B.C., when he was consul and it fell to him to rally the state behind him to deal with the subversive and irresponsible faction led by Catiline, he had found support from the 'sound' elements. But much had passed since 63 B.C. Society was torn to pieces. On the one side were the old aristocratic ideals of rigid morality, state-service, unimpeachable honour and a certain spiritual and physical asceticism – dull and perhaps smug and certainly rare, but of great influence as a reminder and as an ideal; the elder Cato lived again in his grandson who fell by his own hand in the civil wars between Pompey and Caesar. Also there was the people, often of alien blood and of no heritage or memories or pride, ready to be fed at state expense or to sell their vote to unscrupulous politicians. The aristocratic families had to contend among themselves for the magistracies which gave entrance to a career of distinction in the provinces; but those magistracies were too few to satisfy legitimate aspiration or to furnish enough posts to serve the provinces. Traders and bankers and money-lenders furnished capital for any lucrative purpose and supported the politician who would help their interests. The stakes ran high, for big money was made and lost; private and family fortunes had to be restored. Soldiers of the army, which was now a career in itself, were not often seen in Rome, but their invisible legions stood behind their great commanders in the capital. Vast military strength, the resources of great surfaces of the earth, power and prestige and often great personal qualities made these leaders tower in colossal and terrifying proportions above the ordinary citizen, whose lips soon breathed the most damning words of hate which he knew, 'king', 'tyrant', 'autocrat', 'lord and master', 'potentate'.

Strangely enough, Cicero was right; it was indeed possible to muster a public opinion of the sound elements. But ten more years of civil war were necessary to provide a blood-letting and a war-weariness which brought men to destruction or to their senses; and then it was the public opinion not of Rome but of Italy. For the moment greed, corruption, ambition, idleness, intrigue, irresponsibility made Cicero's dream vain. Yet in spite of the times there was culture and idealism and real nobility of aim and conduct; they could not be focused.

Listen to Cicero calling for unity in the parties, unity based on the goodwill of all sound elements in the state. Here are the watchwords of many political parties since, Whigs and Tories and, indeed, revolutionaries.

These men of whom I have spoken, who guide the ship of state – on what objective must they fasten their gaze and set their course? Their objective must be that which is superior to all others, which alone can satisfy the earnest wishes of all men of good sense, of substance, and of loyalty – I mean, a settled and honourable security. Those who aim at that end indeed belong to the party of patriots; those who further it show their high merit and are justly held to be the backbone of their country. A man cannot let himself be carried away by the honour which a policy of vigorous action gains for him if it means that he takes no thought of security; on the other hand he cannot embrace at any cost a security which is repugnant to all standards of honour.

Security and honour – their foundations, or, if you prefer, their constituent parts, which it is the duty of every statesman to watch over and defend, even at the risk of his life, are these: religion and dependence upon divine will, the power of magistrates [*civil authority*], the leadership of the Senate, Law, tradition, justice and its administration, good faith, the provinces, the allied states, the fair name of the Empire, military preparedness, financial stability. To defend and to support ideas so noble and so manifold takes a stout heart, high ability, and inflexible will. For in a citizen-body as large as ours there is a multitude of men who fear the punishment overhanging the wrong-doings of which they know they are guilty and who, therefore, strive after political upheaval and revolution; there are others possessed of an inbred insanity which drives them to glut themselves on civil strife and insurrection; others whose private affairs are involved in such confusion that rather than perish alone they prefer to bring down the state in one general conflagration. Suppose that men of this kind gain for themselves protectors and leaders to promote their evil ambitions; then it is that the seas are lashed into storm, that those who have demanded to take the helm of state into their hands must keep the most vigilant watch, must strain with all their skill and all their stead-fastness to preserve those institutions and ideals which I said just now were the foundation and the constituent parts, and so main-tain their course and seize at last that harbour in which are security and honour. If I told you, gentlemen, that the path was not rough nor steep nor beset with dangers and traps, I should deceive you – and all the more grossly because, not only have I known it all my life, I have had direct experience of it, and more than the rest of you. The armed forces stationed to attack the state are more in number than those which defend it; for it takes only a nod of the head to set in motion the reckless and desperate – indeed of their own initiative they incite themselves against the state. The sound elements rouse themselves more slowly; they overlook the first symptoms of trouble and at the last moment are stirred into belated action by the sheer urgencies of the situation; the pity of it is that, though they are anxious to preserve their security even at the cost of their honour, their own delay and hesitation not infrequently cost them the loss of both.

When returning from the province of Cilicia, of which he had been governor, Cicero had to leave behind at Patrae, on the west coast of Greece, his freedman and friend Tiro, who had fallen ill. Between 3 November and 25 November 50 B.C., Cicero wrote eight letters to him expressing his anxiety. Here is one of them :

I miss you very much and I thought I could bear it more easily, but I simply cannot; and, though it is of great importance to the reception which Rome will give me [*as a returning governor*] that

I should reach the city as soon as possible, still I think I was wrong to leave you. But you seemed to wish not to sail unless you were entirely fit again, and I thoroughly agreed; and I have not changed my mind, if you are still of the same opinion. But if, now that you have taken food again, you think you can catch me up, then it is for you to decide. I sent Mario to you with instructions either to come with you to me as soon as possible, or else, if you decide to stay, to return here immediately. If you can manage it without harm to your health, believe me there is nothing I should like better than to have you with me; but, if you feel that you ought to stay for a little while in Patrae to get well again, believe that there is nothing I want more than that you should be well. If you sail immediately, catch me up at Leucas; but, if you wish to give yourself time to get stronger, take great care that your travelling companions and the weather and the boat are all suitable. One thing I beg of you, my dear Tiro, do not, as you love me, let Mario's arrival and this letter influence you; if you do what is best for your health, you are obeying implicitly my wishes. You are sensible enough to lay that to heart; so pray do. Though I want to see you, my affection wins; affection bids me wait and then see you fully recovered, desire to see you bids me hurry you; therefore choose the former. Your first business is to get well; of your countless kindnesses to me this will give me the most pleasure. (3 November, 50 B.C.)

Marcus Tullius Tiro was Cicero's freedman and his secretary. He was a man of considerable literary attainments himself. According to tradition, he gathered together the speeches and letters of Cicero, and was responsible for their publication; he wrote a life of Cicero.

When Caesar descended upon Rome, the senatorial party hurriedly left the city in order to make feeble efforts to muster resistance. Cicero went into Campania, whence he wrote as follows to his wife and daughter still in Rome:

To Terentia from [*her husband*] Tullius,
to Tullia from her father,
both his most precious;
and to his darling Mother
and sweet sister from Cicero [*his son*]
affectionate greetings.

It is for you, and not only for me, to consider what you ought to do. If he [*Caesar*] is going to come to Rome without threats or violence, it will be all right for you to remain at home, at least for the present; but, if in a fit of madness the man is going to hand over the city to his soldiers to plunder, I am afraid that not even Dolabella's influence will be of any avail to us. I am afraid, too, that we may be cut off already and that you will not be able to get out, however much you wish. Further, you have to take into account – and you can do it best yourselves – whether there are other women of your standing still in Rome; if there are not, you must be very sure that you can remain without giving the impression of being on Caesar's side. As things are now, I don't think you can do better than be with me here – if only we are allowed to retain our position – or else at one of our country houses. Also, there is the danger of scarcity of food in Rome. Please consult Pomponius or Camillus or anyone else you think fit; but above all keep a good heart. Labienus [*who had just deserted Caesar*] has made things a little better for us; it is a help too that Piso has left Rome and thus makes clear his condemnation of Caesar's treachery. Write to me as often as you can, my dearest souls, and tell me what you are doing and what is happening in the city. My brother Quintus and his son, and also Rufus, send you greetings. Good-bye.

Minturnae, 24 January. (49 B.C.)

Terentia and Tullia joined Cicero soon after receiving this letter.

CHAPTER IV

(a) RESTORATION AND THE AUGUSTAN
PRINCIPATE: VERGIL AND HORACE AND LIVY

*In my sixth and seventh consulship, after I had put out the flames of
civil war and by universal consent had become possessed of the control of affairs, I transferred the state from my own power to the will
of the Senate and people of Rome. For this service I received by
decree of the Senate the name of Augustus.*

FROM AUGUSTUS' OWN ACCOUNT OF HIS PRINCIPATE

To explain in a few words the significance of the battle
of Actium which gave Augustus final victory is difficult.
Hellenistic civilization, it will be remembered, was an
amalgam of Greek and Oriental ideas fused together and
spread over the East, especially by the work of Alexander
the Great and his successors. For centuries this civilization
had attracted able Romans, and its influence on thought,
religion, morals, and the material equipment of society
at all levels was great. It had a long past and it enshrined
the massive achievements of centuries of experience. But
alongside this vast tradition, unnoticed for centuries but at
last compelling notice, a new and tentative approach to
the problem of human life – the organization of society,
conduct collective and individual, ideals of character and
behaviour, state-craft and government, ethics and religion
– had painfully been worked out till it had gained confidence in itself and had proved its worth in competition
with other views upon the same problems. This was the
Roman experience, expressed in institutions and standards
and ideals. True, the last century had seen the betrayal of
all these. But not a final or a whole-hearted betrayal –

rather an eclipse due to defect of machinery for the expression of the true instincts of the solid mass of people. The tributary of Roman experience, feeding the river of Mediterranean culture, was thin in volume compared with the Hellenistic stream in its deep-cut bed. But was it of no value? And was it to be lost?

Cleopatra, unlike the modern popular version of her, was of Macedonian and Greek descent, powerful of intellect, a linguist herself able to conduct affairs with foreigners, a student of literature and philosophy, hard-headed in administration, masterful of will and ruthless in carrying it out, not obsessed by the passion of love, which she used as a means, but dominated by the passion for power with which she hoped to achieve her ideal. Alone of the successors of Alexander she dreamt his dream of the fusion of East and West and of the unity of mankind. Her audacious plan was to use a Roman army to subjugate Rome and then, as Empress, divine and supreme, to rule the world; the measure of her influence and her ability can be gauged by estimating the skill and the propaganda needed to persuade to her cause generals of ancient tradition and legionaries of Western origin. The party of Octavianus, to enflame the hatred of the West, might paint her as an Egyptian tyrant, divine embodiment of the animal gods of the Nile, and sunk in every Oriental depravity; but its leaders knew the truth, and did not underrate her. Romans might sometimes hate their enemies; but a special hatred inspires them when they speak of Hannibal and of Cleopatra, a hatred not untinged by fear; and it is fear of something alien, something not Western.

Octavianus, now Caesar Augustus, strove by every measure, direct and indirect, to ensure that the Roman tradition should triumph. He dammed up the flood of

Hellenistic influence, and opened every gate which would admit the Roman genius and its accumulated experience. He rebuilt the temples, he restored standards in morals and conduct, he set a new fashion of work and devotion to duty. He left his mark on every branch of administration; his praise encouraged poets and historians to spread abroad the old Roman ideals and pride in them, his good sense attached to him the middle classes of Italy, still sound at heart, and recruited from them honest administrators and provincial governors. His efforts in large measure succeeded because men wished them to succeed. Eventually they contributed to bring about the unity of mankind – as far as it then could be – from the West by means of Western ideas of human personality and ordered freedom; and those ideas were not conspicuous in the past history of the East.

Augustus moved tentatively towards the constitutional establishment of his power, learning from the fate of Julius Caesar the danger of asserting it too precipitately. Finally, he based it on a combination of the proconsular *imperium*, the 'tribunician power' without the office, and certain privileges which were accorded to him by vote of the people. The proconsular *imperium* gave him command of all the armies, which were now stationed in the provinces on the frontiers; these provinces were governed by nominees of his own; the rest he left to the Senate to administer. The 'tribunician power' gave his person 'sacrosanctity' and his position the appearance of being representative of the people, besides the right of proposing legislation. The special privileges gave him, among other rights, the power of 'commending' candidates at elections. He was chief of the *pontifices*, the college of priests, and held many positions of religious significance. He called himself *Princeps* or 'first citizen', and *Pater Patriae*, 'father of his country'. The consulship he left intact. Routine administration, now thoroughly overhauled and made more efficient by the organization of one 'department' after another, he divided between the Senate and his own civil service, which he built up largely from the middle-class Italians. Thus, he rebuilt the state, using the materials of the Republic, and claimed, with ample justice in theory, that he had 'restored the Republic', while he excelled others only in 'authority' (*auctoritas*), a word with a long and honoured Republican tradition. From the division of function between Princeps and Senate (for it was this rather than a division of power) the new government has since been defined as a 'diarchy' rather than a monarchy; whether it remained so depended, as was to be seen, on the character of the Princeps. But, whatever that character might be, in theory the constitution remained established throughout the period of the Empire on the general lines laid down by Augustus. The Princeps was sincere in his wish that all the elements which he enlisted in the service of the state should function well, and, if well, independently of interference by the Princeps.

Such reconstruction succeeded in its immediate and ultimate results because it was accompanied by a restoration of public confidence. The very thing upon which Cicero so longed in vain to base the Republic was established by the end of Augustus' long Principate. It was established partly because it was already there, though not in the quarters in which Cicero looked for it, partly because of the creative efforts of a Princeps with a superb eye for opportunity and with an insight into the underlying sentiments of the age. This basis was a strong public opinion confident of itself; and Augustus was persuaded that in the Italian people there resided the dynamic energy, the moral reserves, and the sense of heritage and purpose necessary to give the Roman power a new lease of life, to bring about a new age. For this he consciously strove as an architect working to a new design with old materials; and those materials were seen to embody within them possibilities hitherto unsuspected. The work of Vergil and Horace and Livy could never have been conceived and taken shape if the spirit within it had not been inherent in the Roman character; their work answered feelings deep within the Roman consciousness, and brought them to the surface and transmuted them into effort and aspiration. The great national and religious epic of Vergil's *Aeneid*, the canticles of Horace's so-called 'Roman' Odes are no product of 'court patronage', though they certainly received the approval of the Princeps and of his adviser Maecenas.

They are the expressions of a great upsurge of religious feeling, which had long lain under the surface and now welled up on every side. Of this stirring of heart and conscience Horace thought himself to be the prophet or *vates*; under the inspiration of the gods he is the 'voice' – for his own self he sinks – through which regeneration is proclaimed. Before Augustus rebuilt the temples of the gods, Horace had called for their rebuilding; before Augustus announced the great 'Secular Festival' which was to be the threshold of the new age, Horace had announced its advent in terms of Roman religion; Vergil, too, had written the fourth *Eclogue*, which in later times was called the 'Messianic' because its language so resembled that of the Jewish Messianic prophecies. Spiritual regeneration expressed itself chiefly through poetry and the arts of architecture and sculpture. They came first and were the more important; Augustus, following the lead of his prophets Horace and Vergil, tried to achieve similar results through the special medium of the statesman, legislation.

Unfortunately, the greatness of Horace and Vergil as the interpreters of the spirit of the time, which was partly old and partly new, is apparent only after deep study of them. But, if anyone wishes to understand their prophetic message, let him study the *Carmen Saeculare* of Horace or the Sixth Book of the *Aeneid*, or the fourth *Eclogue* or the sculpture of the Altar of Peace, erected in 9 B.C., in the company of a guide who can explain their full religious significance. Here all that can be said is that the great 'Secular Hymn' of Horace was composed to be sung by a choir of boys and girls moving in procession to the temple of Jupiter on the Palatine Hill. It summed up in symbolic form, which trailed manifold associations, the meaning of the 'secular festival'. This festival, decreed by Augustus in 17 B.C. after an interval of 129 years, opened the new age in the spirit of creative hope, not, as formerly, in the spirit of sadness and contrition in which the previous cycle was buried; the new age opened with vows of new devotion to the service of the gods and with prayers for blessings upon men. Girls and boys – that is, those who were to build the new edifice – sang this hymn of the re-dedication of a people. For, if the Roman character has been successfully sketched in the foregoing pages, it will readily be understood that, when the Roman felt sincerely about things of morality or sentiment or value, he expressed them in the language of religion. Opinion may differ now whether he was right or wrong; but there is no logic in arguing that, because his notion of religion was not ours, therefore his sincerity is to be doubted.

Here is a passage from the hymn, though it is almost sacrilege to detach it from its context :

As surely as Rome, O ye gods, is your handiwork, as surely as from
Troy came those armed warriors who settled on the Tuscan shore
– a mere remnant bidden to win a new home and a new city, their
journey finished under your guidance, a remnant which pure-
hearted Aeneas, saved unhurt from blazing Troy to survive his
country, led as by a free highway to a destiny greater than all that
they left behind – so, O gods, to our youth swift to learn grant ways
of righteousness, grant to old age calm and rest, to the race of
Romulus wealth and increase of its sons, O grant all that is glorious ... Already Good Faith and Peace and Honour and the
Modesty of olden days and Virtue so long slighted muster courage
to return, and Plenty with all the riches of its full horn is here for
all to see. Phoebus with his trappings of silver bow, who foresees the
future, who is welcome friend of the nine Muses of Rome, who
with health-giving skill gives new strength to tired limbs – Phoebus
assuredly beholds with just and kindly eyes these towered hills of
Rome and prolongs Rome's greatness and the prosperity of Latium
into yet another cycle and into ages that ever shall grow better.

The *Aeneid* of Vergil was a national and religious epic.
It was epic, for it narrated in verse the doings of Aeneas
and his band of followers in their pilgrimage from Troy
to the Western world in the high enterprise imposed upon
them by a divine will which had its own plans for the
destiny of the world. It was national, for it asserted the
independence of the Roman spirit from the spirit of
Greece and maintained the individual character of
Roman achievement. It was religious, for it expressed in
religious phrase the philosophy of the Roman mind,
fusing the ideal characters of Regulus and Cato and the
rest with the philosophical outlook of Cicero, and pro-
ducing a Roman humanism. The most significant movement of history, therefore, according to Vergil, is the
march of the Roman along the road of his destiny to a
high civilization; for in that destiny is to be found the
valid and permanent interpretation of all movement and
all development. As the Roman alone of all nations had

succeeded under divine guidance, so in the future success
for him alone was assured if he rose to his high calling.
The stately movement of the *Aeneid* progresses throughout its length to this theme, the universal and the ultimate
triumph of the Roman spirit as the highest manifestation
of man's powers.

The *Aeneid* of Vergil views the destiny of Rome, and
that is the destiny of the world, from a transcendental
level. It was the work of another artist, Livy, to view it
from the standpoint of the man of his day who was interested and intelligent enough to read the history of
Rome. Livy traced Rome's history, from the foundation
of the city almost to the time of his death, in one hundred
and forty-two books, of which only thirty-five survive. It
will not create any surprise if the reader is told that it
starts with Aeneas. It is a magnificently conceived prose
epic, with the portraits of the great men of Rome firmly
drawn and the issues of the periods clearly set out. It is
the work of an artist and not of an historian. Livy knows
clearly what his object was in writing history; he held that

this is the most wholesome and faithful effect of the study of history; you have in front of you real examples of every kind of
behaviour, real examples embodied in most conspicuous form;
from these you can take, both for yourself and for the state, ideals
at which to aim, you can learn also what to avoid because it is in-
famous either in its conception or in its issue.

In other words, we are to behold in the pages of his narrative the Romans of old, idealized or at any rate strongly
drawn, and we are to see in them types of morality, and
we are to base our future conduct upon their examples.
Whereas in Vergil's *Aeneid* Aeneas had been taken by the
Sibyl into Hades to see the great Romans yet to be born,
Livy asks us to look back along the Roman portrait

galleries and to be proud and to imitate or to be warned. The conflicts and issues and struggles in the story of Rome are, of course, apparent to him; but they are described in terms of individuals; there are not 'movements' or 'tendencies' or 'forces' at work unattached to men. History is the record of the 'doings of men' (*res gestae*), and the course of history, to Livy, has been determined by Roman men in obedience to Roman gods; to Vergil history is the working out of the destiny of the Roman people seen in the light of eternity. To Horace there was one duty, to proclaim with the inspiration of a prophet that, if Rome did not change her heart and in godliness worship the gods, she would have no history at all; he summoned her to re-dedication. But all these artists express their message, as artists must, in terms of the individual and the special case. That is why Aeneas and the whole company of heroes are worked so hard; they embody ideals; and the Roman mind, and, therefore, the Latin language, prefers not to deal with abstracts, but to see things – movements and tendencies and ideals – as expressed in persons who have lived. Therefore history and moral philosophy, with examples taken from real men, are the branches of thought and literature which most interest the Roman.

The 'Augustan Age' was heralded by an outburst of really sincere feeling, which found sincere expression in the work of three artists, Vergil, Horace, Livy, and of those sculptors who carved the 'religious' sculpture of the Altar of Peace, of which for lack of pictures we cannot speak.

And when Horace and Vergil gave voice to the idea that there was something divine in Augustus, they were sincere and they were Roman.

(b) THE FIRST AND SECOND CENTURIES A.D.

*O Jupiter of the Capitol, O Mars Gradivus, author and stablisher of
the Roman name, O Vesta, guardian of the sacred flame that burns
for ever, and all the gods who have lifted this massive Roman Empire
to the grandest pinnacle of the whole world – upon you in the name
of the people I call aloud in supplication: guard, preserve, protect
this order, this peace, this Emperor: and when he has discharged his
spell of duty upon earth, as prolonged as it can be, then raise up at
the last hour men to succeed him, men whose shoulders shall be no
less broad to bear the burden of world empire than we have seen this
Emperor's to be: and of the counsels of all citizens prosper what is
pleasing to you, and bring to nought what is unpleasing.*

VELLEIUS PATERCULUS

. . . the unmeasured majesty of the Roman peace.

PLINY THE ELDER

Rome is our common fatherland.   MODESTINUS *(Digest)*

In this section it is proposed to treat of certain aspects of
government, organization, social and economic life; there
will be no attempt at consecutive history, and it must be
understood at the outset that some of the statements are
not true of the period as a whole, but only of a part. And
for the purpose of giving a rough indication of the date
we shall refer to the reigns of Emperors, and therefore it
will be an advantage to begin this section with a clue to
their chronology.

Augustus died in A.D. 14. After him came the rest of
the Julio-Claudian line of Emperors, Tiberius, Caius
(Caligula), Claudius, Nero. All these were related, however distantly. On Nero's death in A.D. 68 there followed
a year of conflict between rival commanders of armies,
for Nero had neglected to keep the soldiers' loyalty. From
the conflict Vespasian emerged victor; he was succeeded
by his son Titus, and Titus by his brother Domitian, who
died in A.D. 96. These three compose the Flavian Dynasty.
The next Emperor was the nominee of the Senate, Nerva,

who adopted as his son and successor Trajan, who adopted Hadrian (his second cousin). Hadrian adopted Antoninus Pius, who adopted Marcus Aurelius (his nephew), whose son Commodus succeeded him. The 'Antonine Age' covers the reigns of the three Emperors last mentioned, namely A.D. 138–193. From A.D. 193 to 235 the Severan Dynasty, whose place of origin was Africa, furnished five Emperors of whom Septimius Severus, Caracalla, and Severus Alexander are the most important.

Some of these names, notably Caligula and Nero, have passed into popular knowledge as monsters of depravity, though it knows nothing of the work of Trajan and Hadrian. But, though not all sides of every Emperor will bear scrutiny, the stories must be seen in perspective; Nero's foreign policy, for example, was admirable; Tiberius and Claudius rendered great services (among others) to Roman provincial government and to frontier policy. The truth is that anti-imperial propaganda accounts for many, but by no means all, of the stories retailed by Suetonius and other biographers. But the history of the early Empire, and so of the achievements of the Emperors, is being rewritten by the study of the old records in the light of modern historical criticism and by patient and systematic work on the hundreds of thousands of 'inscriptions' and on papyri and on archaeological sites. And, since reference will sometimes be made to inscriptions, it may be explained that they range from casual scratchings on stone (for example, a soldier scribbling his name and unit on a tile or on the base of a statue) to important official documents such as laws, charters, treaties, decrees : in between fall epitaphs, often giving details of public careers, dedications to gods, which show the distribution of cults, and innumerable other categories.

From them invaluable evidence is forthcoming which
gives hitherto unknown information about such things
as the stations, promotions, movements, and nationalities
of soldiers, municipal government, trade, the spread of
religions, the imperial civil service; indeed, there are few
aspects of life on which light is not thrown.

The collapse of the Republic, as was seen earlier, was
due largely to the inability of the central government to
control provincial governors who were compelled to
extort from the state rewards for their armies. Thus the
military system was at fault. Augustus took steps to put
it right, and we may begin our survey with the Roman
soldier.

The function of the armies henceforth was to police
the frontiers. The force of 25 to 30 legions, about 200,000
men of Roman citizenship, aided by the like number of
'auxiliaries', local levies, was stationed in those provinces
where danger from over the borders might threaten, or
where the inhabitants were not yet romanized : for, as we
shall see, the Roman army was a powerful civilizing influence. Less than half a million men was a small force
for the defence of a frontier line of 10,000 miles. Their
commanders looked directly to the Emperor as their
general-in-chief. The legionary soldier gradually ceased
to be recruited from Italy; Roman citizens from the
provinces volunteered for a service of twenty or twenty-
five years, and their sons regularly took up their fathers'
profession. By military service the 'auxiliary' gained
Roman citizenship for himself and his children, and his
sons could therefore enter the legions. We possess many
examples of the 'discharge papers' bestowing citizenship
and other rights. The permanent camps on the frontiers
attracted civilian settlements; from the settlements grew
townships in which the time-expired soldier settled down

on his gratuity, and frequently held municipal office and achieved local prestige as a benefactor. The Roman soldier spread Roman influence. For he was always more than a soldier; indeed, the equipment which he carried was heavier than the modern infantryman's; he was fighting-man and engineer, he built camps and roads and bridges, he sowed crops and harvested them, he surveyed the country and policed it, his officers set up administrations or supervised local arrangements and dispensed justice. His life lay in the provinces; he may never have seen Rome or Italy; and he would be surprised at the modern picture of him pining for the warm climate of Italy and the life of the capital. But he might arrive there; for the rewards of service and the system of promotion made it possible for the able sons of an auxiliary to reach equestrian and senatorial rank and so to be appointed to the highest military and administrative posts which the imperial system offered.

We cannot describe further: the following extracts will show Roman counterparts of things familiar enough to-day.

After the Emperor Hadrian had reviewed his troops in Africa (A.D. 128), he addressed them at length, and part of what he said was as follows:

You did everything in due order; you covered the whole ground in your manoeuvres; your spear-throwing was neat, though you used the short weapon which is difficult. Most of you were as good with the longer spear. Your jumping was lively today, and yesterday it was swift. If you had fallen short in anything, I would call your attention to it; if you had shone in anything, I would remark on it, but in fact it was the even level of your performance which pleased me. It is clear that my legate Catullinus spares no pains in fulfilling his duties and has omitted nothing. Your own commander too seems to look after you very thoroughly. . . . The jumping will be held on the parade ground of the Commagenian Cohort.

And his address to the Sixth Commagenian Cohort ended thus: 'It is due to the outstanding care which Catullinus has taken that you are what you are today'. It is almost possible to hear the clearing of the throat and the tap of the riding switch upon the military boot.

When the soldier's service was finished, he received a copy of the record, kept in Rome, authorizing his acquisition of rights of Roman citizenship. His copy was on a double tablet (*diploma*).

The Emperor Domitian [*here follow his titles*] granted citizenship to the undermentioned soldiers, cavalry and infantry, of three squadrons and seven cohorts, namely, the Augustan, the Apian, Commagenian, the first Pannonian, the first Spanish, the first Flavian Cilician, the first and second Theban, the second and third Iturean, all under the command of L. Laberius Maximus in Egypt, who have served for twenty-five years or more. To them, their children and their posterity he granted citizenship and the rights of legal marriage with the wives to whom they were married at the time of the grant, or, if they were unmarried, to the wives whom they married thereafter, be it understood in respect of one wife of each soldier.

And then the date and the soldier's name. A *diploma*, found in Bulgaria, belonged to a legionary; it employs the same formula of grant but relates to soldiers 'who had been rendered useless for war and were invalided out before the expiry of their term of service and were given an honourable discharge'. To the individual soldier these papers were valuable. Of the careers and promotions and decorations of individual soldiers we have countless examples. Here is a very short example, found at Turin

[dedicated] to C. Gavius Silvanus, . . . , senior centurion of the VIII Augustan legion, tribune of the II cohort of guards [*in the city of Rome*], tribune of the XIII urban cohort, tribune of the XII cohort of the praetorian guards [*a highly picked and privileged corps*].

In the war in Britain he was decorated by the Emperor
Claudius with four different kinds of badges and decorations which he won as a centurion : 'patron of the colony'
(*i.e. township of Turin*). 'The town council decreed this
monument.'

This leads us to life in the cities. During three centuries
thousands of cities grew into being, and were granted
varying degrees of self-government. Some eleven municipal charters provide us with information about the constitution of the cities ; and it is clear, first, that Rome showed
the greatest respect for local traditions, and, secondly, that
the cities were proud of the privileges so granted to them
and copied the institutions and forms of the capital city.
Thus, the cities had to recognize three elements. First
come the citizens who elected the magistrates in elections
whose freedom was carefully safeguarded. The rules for
voting are as follows :

The presiding officer shall summon the citizens ward by ward to
vote, each ward being summoned at one and the same time, and
they shall record their vote by ballot, each ward in its appropriate
voting-booth. Likewise he shall provide that three of the citizens
of that same municipality shall be assigned to the ballot-box of
each ward, though themselves belonging to a different ward, and
shall act as observers and shall sort the votes; they shall previously
each swear that in all faith and honesty they will keep count of
the votes and return the same. It shall be permitted to candidates
to post a single observer at each ballot-box. The observers posted
by the presiding officer and those posted by the candidates shall
vote in that ward to whose ballot-box they were assigned as observers, and their votes shall be just and valid, as though they had
severally cast them in their own wards.

Preserved under the ashes of Vesuvius, the walls of
Pompeii still bear the election posters of the local elections,
'Vote for Bruttius : he'll keep the rates down'. The various
guilds of workers – woodworkers, muleteers, farmers, and

the like – back their own candidates, and a club of 'late-drinkers' support Vatia 'to a man'.

The second element was the magistrates. The chief magistrates were two in number and, like the consuls at Rome, their power was 'collegial'. We know the qualifications necessary for office; we know also the demands which public opinion made upon them in the way of expenditure on games and festivals.

The third element was the municipal counterpart of the Senate at Rome – the *curia*, usually a hundred in number. This 'order' was usually composed of ex-magistrates. The council was consulted by the magistrates, who were its executive officers. Honours and privileges were given to members of the council, who in return lavished their money upon public works to adorn or to serve the city. And to distinguished men might be given the distinction of being the 'patron' of the township.

The townships called out a loyalty and generosity from rich and poor alike which have scarcely been surpassed since. Roads, temples, theatres, public baths, aqueducts were built and schools were endowed at private expense; humble donations were made for a fountain or a statue. These self-governing cities with an intense pride were established on the edges of the Sahara, in Germany or Rumania where previously no cities stood. Often the hutments which were established outside a camp by civilians catering for the troops were the beginnings of the towns, and many of the most famous cities of Europe, as e.g. Cologne, Mainz, Baden, derived from this origin. The early stage can be seen in this inscription at Troesmis, fifty miles from the mouth of the Danube,

... C. Valerius Pudens a veteran of the v Macedonian legion and M. Ulpius Leontius, magistrate of the settlement, and Tucca Aelius, aedile, gave this gift to the veterans and Roman citizens living [*for the time being, as traders, no doubt*] at the settlement of the v Macedonian legion.

Thus, even before the community had a real name of its own, the ordered government of a township had been set up.

But civic pride had its perils. Cities vied with one another in the splendour of their town-halls or games; budgets failed to balance, and public opinion, taught to enlarge its tastes, demanded more and more from the rich. Office became a burden which few could support. Even within the first two centuries officials from the central government appear, charged with the duty of curtailing local government expenditure. Still later, when the central government was hard pressed to make ends meet, the machinery of the townships offered an easy way for the assessment and exaction of taxes. And so at the end of the third century the proud and independent life of the townships was largely stifled; citizenship was becoming a burden and magistracy was enforced upon the unwilling.

The civil service which was necessary to run so huge an enterprise as the Empire was the creation of the first two centuries. During the Republic the governor's staff in the provinces and the magistrate's staff at home had shouldered the work of administration, and to a great extent these were personal staffs; taxes were collected by 'companies' of collectors who paid over specified sums to the state. Augustus himself had relied to great extent upon the aid of his friends and his 'household', that is to say his freedmen and slaves. The imperial civil service was derived from this practice, at least as regards the lower grades. But it was gradually placed on a different footing, and it was reorganized from time to time, notably by Vespasian and Hadrian. We know the promotions and careers offered at various levels, what were the necessary qualifications for different posts, and how one post led to another. Here is a 'senatorial' career of the second century: P. Mummius Sisenna Rutilianus first held a post in the civil courts; then saw service as military tribune (which at this time was administrative); he gained the quaetorship, tribunate, and praetorship; the praetorship gave entry to certain posts which, in Mummius' case, were command of a legion and then the charge of the treasury. He then became consul, and to him as ex-consul a number of posts were open; those which actually were assigned to him were the charge of an 'alimentary' commission, which will be described later, governorship of Upper Moesia, and finally governorship of Asia. In the same way the 'equestrian' career led to a regular ladder of posts; first, military duties provided a qualifying period; then followed administrative posts, as fiscal agents in the provinces; then secretaryships in government departments at home; and next the prefectures of the imperial post, the fleet, the corn supply, the police, and the like, and finally the prefecture of Egypt and of the praetorian guard. Below these well-defined careers were others composed of a multiplicity of subordinate posts in the imperial service – clerks, shorthand writers, storekeepers, accountants, technicians, of whom we have hundreds of titles. It all sounds very modern, as indeed it was. Minutes were written and passed from department to department and filed. Here is the outline of procedure in a trivial matter: the farmers who have leased the imperial estates at Saepinum complain to Septimianus, the assistant officer in the treasury, that the local magistrates are not using the law to protect their flocks. Septimianus has written to the magistrates 'again and again'; they take no notice. Accordingly Septimianus refers the matter to his superior,

Cosmus, chief fiscal minister. Cosmus sends the papers to the praetorian prefects, who had power over local magistrates. And so the final letter is

From Bassaeus Rufus and Macrinius Vindex, praetorian prefects, to the magistrates of Saepinum. We send a copy of a letter received from Cosmus. We warn you to stop injuring the men who have leased the estate and thus inflicting a loss on the treasury; otherwise we shall inquire and punish.

With an army to protect it and a civil service to administer it, the Empire gave freedom of travel and of trade; there was no colour bar, and there were no tariffs, only harbour dues. As the elder Pliny said, 'The might of the Roman Empire has made the world the possession of all; human life has profited by the exchange of goods and by partnership in the blessings of peace'. Imperial couriers, aiming at certainty rather than speed, covered about fifty miles a day; but we know of faster journeys, as for example from Rheims to Rome in nine days (1,440 Roman miles). Rome to Alexandria was a voyage of about three weeks; it took about a year for a merchantman to go to India and back, with time for turning round the cargo. The produce of one country was available to another; the raw materials of the Northern provinces, minerals, timber, hides, were conveyed to the Mediterranean, till these provinces set up factories of their own; the potteries of Gaul and Germany captured the trade of the Italian potteries. Glass was made at Tyre and in Egypt, but soon it was manufactured in Normandy and shipped to Germany and Britain. In the East, Alexandria linked the Mediterranean lands with Egypt and the Far East; corn, granite, silks, marble, ivory, precious metals, papyrus, linen were among the produce of Egypt. The great Roman roads made easy the conveyance of goods, both raw materials and manufactured, and the water-

ways were worked industriously by shippers. Nor were the
lands beyond the Empire left out of account; an adven-
turous Roman is said to have reached the Baltic; Strabo,
the geographer, says that in a year one hundred and
twenty ships would leave for India. In the time of Hadrian
China was reached by sea, and Marcus Aurelius sent a
trade mission thither, of which there is independent evidence in Chinese records. The story of commerce and
exploration in Roman times is fascinating in its scope and
in its detail.

The movement of men was as extensive as the movement of goods. Soldiers and traders, officials and civil servants, travellers for pleasure, students and wandering
philosophers and preachers, commercial agents, the
couriers of the imperial post and of banks and shipping
offices – these and many more thronged the roads and the
sea-routes. The great cities, especially on the coast, were
cosmopolitan in their population. Syrians and Greeks,
Spaniards and Africans and scores of other nationalities
were mingled in the towns and served in the same offices
and departments or factories or private households. The
satirists are never tired of calling attention to the 'Orontes'
– a river of Syria – 'pouring its waters into the Roman
Tiber'. Men of alien origin brought with them their customs and superstitions and cults and moral standards; and
Eastern religions spread far into the West, and often were
adapted and absorbed by native religions, preserving titles
and elements of ritual grafted on to one another in curious
variety. In course of time distinction of race was largely
forgotten, and men of provincial nationality rose to eminence in literature, and letters, and soldiering, and government. Livy came from Padua, Seneca, and his brother
Gallio, and Lucan, from Cordova, Columella from Cadiz,
Martial and Quintilian from Spain, Fronto and Apuleius

from Africa; in the third century, as we shall see, the Emperors themselves came from anywhere but Italy.

One powerful cause of the mingling of nations is to be found in slavery. During these centuries slavery was profoundly altered. As wars of expansion ceased, captives were scarcer, and barbarians made bad slaves; the economic fallacy of slavery in agriculture and industry became clearer and standards of humanity were raised. From the lowest motives of freedom it was discovered that, the nearer the lot of a slave approached to that of a free man, the more useful he was. The Romans disliked retail trade and the routine of business, and slaves performed these tasks for them; the slaves themselves were often more skilled than their masters. Slaves had always been allowed to have property of their own, and in the early Empire this property was often considerable. The elaborate law dealing with slaves' property shows how they could conduct business with free men, and it is clear that slaves owned land, property, ships, interests in business concerns, even slaves of their own, and that their rights were protected by law. When Augustus started his own civil service, he staffed it with slaves and freedmen; their status improved and the work of the townships was carried on by men who were strictly owned by the state or the municipality. The position of the slave was often enviable; he had opportunities without responsibilities, and some slaves preferred to remain as they were. Of course, cases of cruelty were common enough; but legislation restricted it as public opinion made itself felt, and masters like Pliny were kind enough, not to say indulgent. Many a slave was the trusted friend of his master. Indeed, slavery comes nearest to its justification in the early Roman Empire: for a man from a 'backward' race might be brought within the pale of civilization, educated and trained in a craft or profession, and turned into a useful member of society. 'Thank heaven for slavery,' cries a freedman in the *Satiricon* of Petronius, 'it made me what you see me now.'

It is also true that the institution was harmful to society, both morally and economically.

The slave could look forward to freedom, and Augustus found the freedman class increasing and the free population decreasing. In his opinion, manumission – and manumission turned the ex-slave into a Roman citizen eligible for any and every post – was doing harm : and he reorganized the methods of granting freedom, instituting a status of lesser rights as a kind of probation. His aim was to rejuvenate society by admitting to it the best elements of slavery, and those elements were to be admitted to the highest circles and the most important positions.

Among freedmen were some of the richest and most powerful and most notorious men of the early Empire. Many rose to the secretaryships of government departments and to provincial posts of various kinds. Licinus was originally a Gaul, slave of Julius Caesar ; he rose to be procurator of Gaul, where he amassed for himself a fortune 'with the greed of a barbarian while enjoying the dignity of a Roman' ; Felix, procurator of Judaea (see Acts xxiii, xxiv) was another freedman. The influence of Narcissus and Nymphidius on the court, and their rise and fall, cannot here be described. But the more humble freedman often made a valuable contribution to the townships of the Empire; he, too, like the veteran soldier, found opportunity for acquiring esteem and influence in the town in which he had worked as a slave. Freedmen pay for public works, make bequests, and endow institutions. Polycarpus and Europe, slaves of Domitia, daughter of Nero's general Corbulo, built a temple at their own expense : when they became freed, they gave to the township a sum of money, the interest on which was to be devoted to the upkeep of the temple and to the cost of an annual bequest on Domitia's birthday. In all the provinces the story of generosity is the same. And the town councils voted in return dignities and honours and privileges.

Of course, social changes of this kind have their risks; ostentation, gross manners, avarice, corruption, and vulgarity could not be avoided, and the satirists, and particularly Petronius, expose them. None the less, the 'compulsory initiation into a higher culture' achieved by slavery found much justification in the record of freedmen and their posterity. In later ages few families could claim total freedom from servile blood at some point in their pedigrees, and many a man traced his birth back to a mythological ancestor in order to draw attention away from intervening generations.

Before this topic is left some examples may be given.

An epitaph of three lines of modern print (such is the brevity of Latin) gives the following information about Oriens and his relations. He was a slave owned by the town of Saepinum and was engaged in executive duties; with his wife he érected a monument to his father L. Saepinius Oriens, who belonged to an 'order' of local dignitaries of the town, and also to L. Saepinius Orestes, his brother, who was a magistrate in the same town. And they probably all 'knew' each other socially, as the epitaph suggests. The father was freed after the birth of Oriens, and before the birth of Oriens' brother; hence the difference in status.

Petronius, who gives a most vivid, though perhaps exaggerated, picture of life among freedmen, puts the following description into the mouth of one of his characters:

They are very juicy people. That one you see lying at the bottom of the end sofa has his eight thousand. He was quite a nobody. A little time ago he was carrying loads of wood on his back. People do say – I know nothing, I have only heard – that he pulled off a goblin's cap and found a fairy hoard. If God makes presents, I am jealous of nobody. Still, he shows the marks of his master's fingers, and has a fine opinion of himself. So he has just put up a notice on his hovel: 'This attic, the property of Gaius Pompeius Diogenes, to let from the 1st July, the owner having purchased a house' [translation by M. Heseltine].

Another guest at the same banquet had held a cool million in his grasp; but things had not gone well; the company's pot had gone off the boil. Yet his trade was flourishing once; he was an undertaker. He dined like a king; more wine was spilt under his table than many a man had in his cellars.

Finally, a very brief account may be given of the 'clubs' which were organized by slaves and freedmen and the poorer free men. These clubs, which might include men of each status, combined a religious cult with the amenities of a social or 'dining' club, and often made provision for the funerals of members – church, social club, craft-guild, and funeral society. Again, the Romans' genius for 'order' asserts itself, as the rules and minutes which we possess abundantly show. Officers are elected who on appointment take the oath and on resignation render up accounts; new members are advised to read the rules and expected to pay their subscriptions. The rules, which are couched in the language of Roman law, lay down conditions about entrance fee, subscriptions, funeral benefits, expenses of those who attend the funeral, about the kind of fare and wine to be provided at 'club' dinners, about complaints and about the standard of behaviour expected. All very trivial, but of no little significance.

One point of significance is the testimony to a wide-spread desire for sociableness. The Empire was a large conception, too large for most. The township offered a lesser loyalty within the larger loyalty, but a still smaller unit was needed. The well-to-do had their circles, by no means exclusive; those of lesser means with common interests or occupations created their own society. The individual wanted a means to realize himself as an individual. And not only in his lifetime. Nothing is more remarkable than the craving of the individual, rich and poor, to perpetuate his memory by a bequest, or a tombstone, or a line or two on the urn which would hold his ashes. Many a man erected his tomb in his lifetime and left a sum to provide for its upkeep. 'While still Vitalis,' writes Vitalis himself with a jest on his name, 'and enjoying vitality, I built myself a tomb, and every time I pass I read with these two eyes my own epitaph.' Not all are so light-hearted. There is in general a pathetic hopelessness, and a more pathetic craving for hope in these legends, which we possess in thousands. Some blatantly protest that there is no life to come; others tentatively suggest its possibility; only in Christian epitaphs is there a positive assertion of certainty.

In earlier chapters it was pointed out that the characteristically Roman virtue of *pietas* expressed and strengthened family affection and family ties. We may see one manifestation of *pietas* in the care for the maintenance of children embodied in the institution known as the *alimenta*, though some writers have regarded increase of population and recruitment for the army as the motives which inspired its adoption by the state.

Private generosity sometimes secured for the children of a particular town a maintenance allowance of food, and a gift of money when they reached the age at which they could earn. The cost was met from the interest derived from a capital sum donated to the township. The Emperor Nerva adopted a similar plan in founding the 'state' maintenance allowances for 5,000 Italian children, as a beginning. The system was extended by later Emperors, especially Trajan, Marcus Aurelius, Septimius Severus, and it disappeared in the reign of Diocletian. Briefly the scheme was this : the treasury made loans to farmers, who rendered a return of the value of their land; the loan was not more than about one-twelfth of the capital value. The farmer paid the interest at 5 per cent to his local township, which was bound to spend it on the maintenance of children of the town. If the interest was not paid, the town could distrain upon the farm. Thus the imperial treasury found the capital to aid Italian agriculture; the farmer had the use of the capital, but was not allowed to borrow recklessly; the town received the interest based upon good security; the children received food and clothing. Boys and girls benefited, though the allowance for girls per month was slightly less than for boys, and they ceased to qualify at an earlier age. We know that the system operated in forty cities in Italy, and a department of the civil service administered it; we also know that private generosity still flowed in spite of the parallel system of the state. The Emperors were proud of the scheme; *Alim. Italiae* appears on the coins of Trajan, and Trajan's Arch at Beneventum shows him greeted by four women, one with a baby in her arms, and by two Roman citizens, one with a boy on his shoulders, the other with a boy at his side. The women, no doubt, symbolize cities.

The legends on coins to which reference has just been made perhaps call for a paragraph on one aspect of ancient coinage. It was far more interesting than our own, for the types were frequently changed, and the legends and the pictures were chosen to suit the times. Thus the Emperor could impress upon the public the significance of a recent event, or he could prepare opinion for a project, or he could stiffen morale by focusing attention on ideals. In fact, the coinage not only repairs some gaps in the historical evidence and corroborates the rest, but also provides a commentary and an interpretation, not less welcome or important for being official. When Antoninus Pius was preparing his subjects for the nine-hundredth anniversary of the foundation of Rome, he issued medallions showing the landing of Aeneas upon the shores of Italy. The victory over the Parthians and the recovery of the 'lost standards' is duly recorded upon gold coins issued by Augustus. The fall of Jerusalem in A.D. 70, the bridging of the Danube in Trajan's Dacian wars, Hadrian's tour of the provinces, the adoption of a successor by a reigning Emperor and so his recommendation to the world at large, specific acts of imperial generosity or state-craft, as for example the *alimenta* – this is the kind of event recorded. Prosperity is acclaimed or invited; if there had been civil war, 'Concordia' as a legend would record its end, or even a hope that it might end. 'Eternal Rome' is a prayer; the Emperor portrayed as peace-bearer or the 'restorer of liberty' is an intimation of his aims. In the third century, Emperors, by associating themselves on coins with the cult of a particular deity, signified also their association with the policy of their predecessors who had also identified themselves with that cult. At the time when Diocletian persecuted the Christian Church, his coins bore the inscription 'Genius of the Roman People', and thus reasserted faith in the mystical mission of pagan Rome.

From these serious matters we turn for a moment to the lighter side of life. The pleasures and amusements of children remain much the same throughout the ages. Dolls and toy carts and pet animals and similar playthings were common. Ball games played in a court or against a wall, ball games played with sticks or racquets were a usual pastime with boys and a favourite form of exercise with men. Games with stones or nuts or knucklebones resembled the game of 'jacks' which still lingers in English villages. There were games with dice, and 'board' games played with pieces according to elaborate rules. That games of those days were not unlike those of modern children may be guessed from the following description of another game given by a second-century writer. The game is as follows:

From the shingle you pick a well-shaped pebble worn smooth by the tossing of the waves; you hold the pebble horizontally in the fingers and send it spinning just over the waves, keeping it flat and as low as possible, so that when thrown either it grazes the surface of the water and leaps off as it skims along with easy flight, or else it shaves the tops of the waves and flashes out of them and reappears lifted above them in one leap after another. That boy proclaims himself the winner whose pebble travels furthest and makes the most jumps.

The public amusements of the adult Roman are another matter. The so-called 'games' generally included gladiatorial shows, wild-beast fights, chariot-racing, and theatrical shows. It is probable that the cruel contests between men and men or men and beasts were a legacy to Rome from the Etruscan domination, though throughout the Mediterranean there existed native festivals and sports of similar kind. Nothing can mitigate the vulgarity and beastliness, the revolting horror of these shows; it is remarkable how educated men, whose whole sympathies were on the side of humanity and decency, were prepared, when convention or ambition demanded it from them as politicians or successful generals, to provide entertainments whose barbarity shocked them as individuals. On the details of these pleasures we need not dilate; suffice it to say that they were organized on a colossal scale and occupied an important place in the thoughts and expectations of the city populations.

Neither it is necessary to dilate upon the degree to which pleasures of the table were carried in some epochs of Roman life. The delights of fine and skilful preparation of food, of the chef's work as a fine art, would perhaps provoke less criticism in an age which, though it lives on memories, has not yet entirely forgotten. But there was an element of gluttony in some circles, and not only in the circles of the freedmen of Trimalchio's type. And there are many other revolting sides of Roman life, as indeed in the life of fifth-century Athens or the Golden Age of Florence and Venice or the great days of Paris and London. No one assessing the character of a culture must lose sight of its bad features; a vein of cruelty and sensuality ran through the Roman character.

In the meantime, amid the social and political and economic changes of the early empire, what had happened to the old Roman virtues, the sense of duty to state and to family and to friends and of loyalty to moral standards? In spite of the extravagances of fashion and licence which surrounded them, the virtues persisted, less rugged perhaps, more humane but none the less real and pervasive. They flourished chiefly in the country in the cultivated society of men like Pliny, in the farmstead from which sprang men such as the Emperor Vespasian, an Emperor great through his plain and honest common sense, in the villages and country towns of the provinces now affected by Roman ways of life. When Vespasian took a holiday, he went back to the Sabine farmhouse of his forefathers, which was kept unaltered. The letters of Pliny reveal a society whose members were untouched by the excesses of the capital, though many of them were men whose work and interests brought them into closest touch with its life. The men are interested in their work, their house and land, their literary pursuits, and, perhaps, above all, their friends; the women embody the virtues of the wife and mother and are interested in literature, in their husbands' pursuits, and in their family; the children are brought up in the healthy occupations of the countryside, and are trained in an unoppressive obedience and a natural respect. The foundation of this calm and healthy routine of life seems to be the life of the home and the mutual regard and affection of friends. Whereas we find in the letters of Cicero a vivid commentary on contemporary political life, in Pliny's letters we have a picture of that placid social life which was typical of the 'Antonine Age' which immediately followed the age of Pliny – and a picture drawn by one who found in the small things of daily occupation an absorbing interest and pleasure. Pliny himself had a public career; he pleaded in the law-courts, he went through the various stages of the imperial service; he was governor of the province of Bithynia in the reign of Trajan. He had his vanities but they were harmless; he and his friends were passionately devoted to literature; they took infinite trouble with their own compositions, speeches and poetry, for they suspected that literature was dying and they tried to keep it alive. But above all they valued a sense of humanity, and the breadth and generosity of their outlook is the most conspicuous feature of their intercourse. Perhaps the letter which Pliny wrote to a friend about the death of the daughter of Fundanus will give a hint.

I am very sad as I write to you, for our friend Fundanus' youngest daughter has died. I never saw anything more jolly than this girl, more lovable or more deserving not only of long life but almost of immortality. She was not yet thirteen years old, and she had all the sense of an old woman, the dignity of a mother, the shy innocence of maidenhood with the sweetness of a young girl. How she used to cling to her father's embrace, and throw her arms round the necks of his friends in her affectionate and shy way. She loved her nurses, her teachers and tutors, each in return for what they had done for her. Her reading, how eager and intelligent it was, her play how restrained and circumspect! And think of the self-control, the patience, the courage with which she bore her last illness. She did all that her doctors told her to do; she tried to cheer up her sister and father, and by strength of will she kept her weak body going as its strength slipped away. Her will lasted to the very end, unbroken by her illness or by fear of the death which was to give us all the more urgent cause to miss her and mourn her. Her death was indeed a bitter sorrow; its blow was made even worse by the moment of its coming. She was engaged to an excellent young man; her wedding day had been arranged, the invitations had been sent out. And all that joy was turned to grief. I cannot tell you what a stab it gave me to hear Fundanus – grief discovers such distressing things – giving orders that the money which he was going to spend on bridal clothes and pearls and jewellery should be used on incense and unguents and perfumes needed for the funeral. He is a learned and reflective man, the sort of man who has given all his life to serious study and pursuits; now he rejects with loathing all the counsel he has so often heard and given, and, driving out of his mind every other ideal, he is utterly given up to thoughts of family affection. You will understand him, indeed you will admire him if you reflect what he has lost. He has lost a daughter who mirrored no less his character than his features and expression; with a remarkable resemblance she bodied forth her father's very self. If you write to him about this very real grief, be sure you don't write him a letter urging him to pull himself together or expressed too vigorously; write him a gentle and affectionate letter. An interval of time will do much to make him more ready to accept your comfort. A wound which is still raw shrinks from the doctor's touch, then it endures it and then actually wants it: in the same way grief when fresh rejects and shuns attempts at consolation; soon it desires them and finally acquiesces in them if they are gently made.

And here is Pliny writing to his wife Calpurnia.

Never have I chafed more impatiently under my engagements which have prevented me from accompanying you on your journey

to Campania to convalesce and from following immediately after
you. For at this moment I particularly want to be with you; I want
to believe the evidence of my eyes and see what you are doing to
look after your strength and your little self, whether in fact you
are enjoying to the full the peace and the pleasures and the richness
of the place. Even if you were strong, your absence would still dis-
quiet me. For, when you love people most passionately, it is a strain
and a worry not to know anything about them even for a moment.
But, as things are, the thought of your absence, together with your
ill-health, terrifies me with vague and mixed anxieties. I imagine
everything, my imaginings make me afraid of everything; and, as
happens when you are afraid, I picture the very things I pray most
may not happen. I beg you therefore all the more earnestly to be
kind to my fears and to send me a letter, or even two letters, every
day. While I am reading it, I shall worry less: when I have
finished it, my fears will at once return.

And another letter ends with the words 'write as often
as you can – though the delight of getting your letters is a
sheer torment'.

From letters of this kind – and more cannot be quoted –
it is not difficult to infer what were the manners and the
ideals of the society from which they spring.

Of the statesmanship and home and foreign policy of
Emperors, of the society of the educated and well-to-do, of
letters and thought and philosophy and the manifold cults
and rituals, of moral and spiritual aspirations and disap-
pointments, of the majestic wisdom of Roman law and the
follies and cruelties and depravities of individual men and
women, of the growth of humanity and humanism and the
process of civilization – of all this and more this chapter
can give no impression. But nowadays the popular imagination is too ready to identify Rome with the barbarities
of the arena, which are true enough, though forgetting
their modern counterparts, or with the extravagances of
the imperial court at its worst moments. But the Roman
Empire is not justly interpreted thus; and, if the few

features of life in the first two centuries which have been briefly indicated here are considered with imagination, perhaps something of the immensity of the subject, and something of its fascination, may be dimly seen.

CHAPTER V

WHAT THE ROMANS WROTE ABOUT

The hours which others give up to looking after their own concerns, to public festivals and holidays, to various pleasures and even to rest for mind and body – which others devote to dinner-parties starting early in the evening, to the dice-board and to ball games – these hours I have taken for the incessant pursuit of studies of this kind. And who would criticize me for this or with any justice be angry with me?   CICERO

THIS chapter does not contain an outline history of Latin literature. It attempts merely to indicate the kinds of things in which the Roman writers and their readers were interested; some topics as, for example, philosophy, are treated more fully in other chapters.

At the outset certain points must be made. First, it must be remembered that the Latin literature which survives is the merest fragment of the whole; all the works of certain authors, whom we would gladly read, have been lost, and inferior authors have been preserved. Though on the whole we are fortunate in the survivals, students of history would like to have details of economic life, particularly in the provinces, and the official records which we know were kept; students of philology would like more specimens of the language of daily life, and students of literature bewail the loss of authors whose works would give continuity to the development of particular genres, as for example drama and lyric poetry.

Again, it is not easy to indicate briefly what was the standard of literacy, or the size of the reading public. Inscriptions, to which reference has been made on page

89, were set up by rich and poor alike; and there is little point in an artisan putting up an epitaph if relations were incapable of reading it. The election posters placarded on the walls at Pompeii, shop signs, and public notices all imply a public which could read. Varro in his treatise on farming recommends that certain main rules should be written out and put up where all on the farm can read them. The papyri of Egypt suggest that most people could read and write; soldiers write letters home, and everyday household documents abound. Sometimes it is true that a soldier employs a letter-writer, but that was not unknown in France in the war of 1914–18; and sometimes an inscription in the catacombs carries a little picture to help the illiterate to identify it : for example, the grave space of a little girl, by name Porcella, bears a rough picture of a 'piglet'. But on the whole ability to read was common.

The book trade flourished; copies of histories, poems, or the last public speech of Cicero were eagerly bought in the provinces, and manuscripts were sent from friend to friend. Horace and Vergil became schoolbooks in their lifetime and appropriate quotations from Roman poets are embodied in epitaphs (though this does not imply that those responsible had necessarily read Vergil or Ovid!). Shorthand writers, using symbols easily mistaken for those used today, took down public speeches, as for example those of Cicero 'Against Catiline'; they were employed by authors like Pliny the Elder, who dictated to shorthand writers his voluminous notes on natural history, or St Jerome, who dictated his commentaries on the Scriptures. It is probable that in many areas a higher standard of literacy and a greater knowledge of literature prevailed at certain periods than in those same areas today.

Yet it should not be inferred that Latin and Greek were the only languages. Native languages flourished in spite of

the Roman Empire; St Augustine, for example, as bishop
of Hippo in Africa, found it necessary to engage priests
who knew Punic, and this though Africa had been a province for centuries.

Thirdly, Latin literature in its 'best' periods was addressed on the whole to a highly educated audience, generally conversant with Rome, her history and institutions,
and with Greek ideas and literature. And 'audience' is
used advisedly, for it must not be forgotten that all books
were intended to be read aloud very much more than is
the practice nowadays; and herein partly lies the reason
for a certain oratorical element which runs through a great
portion of Latin literature.

Finally, it must not be assumed that, because the Empire was Roman, important works were all written in
Latin. On the contrary; Greek was the language of the
Eastern Mediterranean, and as much Greek as Latin literature was written throughout the period of the Roman
Empire, both pagan and Christian. There are whole tracts
of Roman history for which we are largely dependent on
the work of historians writing Roman history in the Greek
language; and there are some types of literature, as, for
example, the imaginative stories and conversations of
Lucian (born about A.D. 125), to which nothing quite
corresponds in Latin. But in this chapter we are concerned
only with Latin literature. Yet again a warning is necessary. The Roman of Rome itself was one thing; the
Roman, who was a Spaniard or African or an Italian,
was also a 'Roman' and wrote in Latin. But by virtue of
his race he might be very different in temperament and
feeling: he might have, therefore, different things to say;
he might express them in his own way and alter the Latin
language itself to suit his own genius. Latin literature
manifests different strains deriving from many racial

sources, blended in varying proportions, but fused always into something that is still Roman and Latin.

The Roman character sketched in the introductory chapter of this book prepares us for the general characteristics of Latin literature. It is serious-minded; it is very conscious of Rome and her past and future; it is interested in human purposes. These purposes take the form of man's behaviour to man, that is, morality, or of man's activities to satisfy practical needs, as, for example, agriculture. Thus the moralizing and didactic strain is strong; the aim of literature was to teach, and it is not surprising that Roman education consisted largely of the study of literature, Latin and Greek. All this does not mean that Latin literature is incapable of lightheartedness, or wit, or sarcasm, or parody, nor that it is oblivious of human passion, or devoid of sensitiveness of feeling, or unaware of natural beauty. Yet, though there are elements of the romantic in Roman literature, somehow the romantic (in spite of its name) seems to be not strictly Roman, but to be due to the Italian or provincial strains of which we have spoken. The Roman strain wins by sheer weight, yet not by force; for the Italian or provincial writer has willingly become Roman.

On the highest plane the actions of men are the subject-matter of epic. To the Roman, epic is, of course, the epic of Rome; Rome is the heroine inspiring Romans to heroic deeds to fulfil her destiny. On exactly the same level is history, for such a history as Livy's 'From the founding of the city' is simply prose epic; the heroine in Livy is Rome as surely as in the *Aeneid*, and Roman portraits are drawn for the men of the day to imitate. In verse, Naevius (born about 260 B.C.) described the gigantic struggle between Rome and Carthage, and Ennius (born 239 B.C.) took the broader canvas of the whole of Roman history to his day; before Livy there was a 'great crowd of historians' and there were many after him. But in epic poetry and in history conceived as epic all predecessors led up to Vergil and Livy, and thereafter all looked back to them; they were the masters in showing the Roman at his noblest in action and character, and they perfected the manner and the language for the purpose.

On the plane of everyday life there is no pageantry, and conduct and character are less heroic. They may be shown in the published speeches of statesmen, in the Senate or in semi-political trials; letters display actions and the thoughts and motives which inspire them, till the writer's character and the condition of his society are laid bare for a discerning reader. To the Romans moral essays were of great appeal; discourses on such themes as friendship, duty, standards of right and wrong. The same practical lessons could be driven home in a medium which the Romans perfected, namely satire, in which, as Quintilian said, they 'had it all their own way'. Here men and manners were held up for admiration or scorn : foibles, weaknesses, mannerisms, and inconsistencies were exposed, as in the satires and 'epistles' of Horace, or lashed by scourges of ridicule and invective by Juvenal, whose moral indignation nevertheless does not always ring true.

The same didactic purpose naturally produced manuals of instruction as, for example, the treatises of Varro and Columella on farming, or the survey of the water-supply of Rome by Frontinus, the head of the government department concerned, or 'On the profession of Arms', by Vegetius. Even in them the moral element is not lacking; for example, farming, to be successful, implies certain qualities of character and in turn produces them; and this aspect is never forgotten.

Abstract philosophical speculation never attracted the

Roman, and he did not push moral philosophy, which really appealed to him, back to its metaphysical implications. In the same way he neglected natural science, as a science, though collections of observations and of recorded lore were made, besides the handbooks of medicine or veterinary science or botany and the like.

Tragedies and comedies were written and acted; the comedies of Plautus and Terence and some tragedies of Seneca survive and have exerted great influence on European drama. But on the whole, drama was not a typically Roman form of literature. The Roman never overcame his objection to acting, and a drama which is not written for acting does not flourish. Like the Puritan he thought it wrong to surrender one's own personality and to assume another's: it offended against a sense of 'gravity'. The more successfully it was done, the more it led to emotional and, therefore, moral instability; and the reputation of actors was not high.

The poetry of personal feeling and of passion does not bulk largely in the remains of Latin poetry; there are supreme examples of it in Vergil, in Catullus, and here and there in Propertius. But it is not typically Roman. Nor is the literature of pure imagination Roman – the fairy story, the highly romantic novel, the imaginary visit to the moon, or to far-off lands. These are the products of Greek authors writing in Roman times, though Ovid, writing in Latin verse, had already created, in his *Metamorphoses*, a romantic world of fable and had described it in effortless narrative.

Though there are many biographies in Roman literature, notably Suetonius' lives of the Emperors, and above all Tacitus' masterpiece, 'The Life of Agricola', who was his father-in-law, there is no volume of 'memoirs' or 'recollections' on a full scale. Naturally speeches and letters and essays must contain elements of autobiography. Letters may be almost a diary for a particular period; those of Pliny and Cicero and Fronto and Marcus Aurelius and Symmachus often record trivial happenings or reflections, the day-to-day life of very human men. But no full-dress autobiography has come down to us; and certainly there is nothing in pagan literature at all comparable with 'The Confessions' of St Augustine.

Through Latin literature there runs a vein of oratory; there is always a deliberate heightening of effect to secure the sympathetic attention of the readers, or rather audience. Rhetoric had been a favourite study in the academies and universities in the Hellenistic age; it had languished in artificiality because it had been denied the sincerity and vigour imparted by a genuinely free political life. It had become academic in the worst sense of the word, but it was still valued, particularly by the phil-Hellene circles in Rome. It formed part of an advanced education. But there may also have been other reasons for the liking of the Romans for oratory. It may have been due perhaps to their natural tendency to moralize, to hold up moral patterns. You cannot argue your hearer into accepting a moral ideal, for an ideal is not a matter of intellect or reason. You can only hope to win his agreement and approval by presenting it skilfully and winningly, by stirring his feeling, even by overwhelming him in a torrent of surging emotion till he yields to its appeal. Because Roman literature is at heart concerned so much with what is not a matter of reason, it has recourse to something more than argument cold and unadorned, namely rhetoric.

Moreover, the nursery of oratory is to be found in the political assemblies and law courts. As Rome grew, the issues to be decided in these places became more important, till decision might affect in principle the fortunes of the whole Mediterranean. The platform was Imperial Rome; the statesman or lawyer, impressed by the gravity of his responsibility, rightly felt that the presentation of his case and the language employed must be appropriate. And so oratory became part of the education of boys who might eventually pass into public life; and through education and the growth of tradition it affected to some degree most of Latin literature.

This brief summary suggests that Latin literature was drab and unexciting: a reader who knows the literature might well protest, and he would be right. For it leaves out all the aspects which reveal the Roman as intensely varied and interesting and inspiring in spite of himself – the tenderness and the sensitive pity and the dramatic urgency of Vergil, the exquisite workmanship of the Odes of Horace, where a tremor of judgement would be disastrous, the fluid facility of Ovid, the passion of Lucretius, the self-revealing artlessness of Catullus. It omits the Roman's love of the countryside and its moods, the warmth of affection shown in letters between friends, the love and gratitude of son towards father, the intense interest in literature for its own sake. 'Humanity' and 'the humanities' are in origin Roman ideas; and Latin literature reflects a varied but disciplined humanity.

To convey the quality of a language to those who are not familiar with it is impossible; yet a reader might justly ask for some hint which may give a not erroneous impression. Latin sees things in concrete form; it deals in pictures rather than in abstractions and it is careful of the order in which it presents its pictures to the hearer. Sometimes English people are puzzled that the Latin sentence should regularly adopt the order 'subject, object, verb'. The Roman hearer liked to be presented first with the two terms and then with the relationship linking those terms rather than with one term, then the relationship, then the other term. Words denoting abstracts are used more sparingly than in English; the weight of meaning is borne by the verb. Whereas English might round off a paragraph with 'such were the considerations which led to his decision to ...' Latin says 'for these reasons he decided to ...' Latin delights in strong contrasts, in the balance of ideas logically opposed. It may be brief and epigrammatic, and is admirably fitted for inscriptions. It can build up long periods with perfect clarity. It achieves clarity by the careful presentation of ideas in their logical order, or in the order of the time of the happening of the events, and these two orders are in essence the same; thus, the statement of a cause (though in a grammatically subordinate clause) precedes in order the statement of the effect of the cause. The full-mouthed periods of the orator may roll easily to their conclusion; the simplest sentence composed of the simplest words is equally natural. In Greek, words may spontaneously coalesce to form compounds which are expressive and well-sounding; Latin has no such gift. It can clothe the trite and the pedestrian with a sonority more deserving of a better theme; it can condense wisdom into an impressive brevity, and often, when Latin has said a thing, it cannot be better said. In vocabulary it is less rich than Greek with its multitude of compounds; but its words can carry associations and suggest ideas which no paraphrase can convey. Latin words do not contain as many short syllables as Greek; the dance of the Greek hexameter is replaced by the majesty of the Latin. The flexibility of Latin has allowed it to be adapted for all purposes through the ages – for liturgy and Christian theology, for learned works in natural science and philosophy, for pamphlets and correspondence, limericks, newspapers, encyclicals, and every purpose which learning and social intercourse and civilized life embrace. Its living presence, as regards words and ideas, in the language of Europe is a commonplace.

But a literature cannot be described: translation can do a little to convey something of its character: short extracts may misrepresent even that little. None the less, four passages are given here in the hope that one or two of the points made in this chapter may be made clearer.

The first passage, taken from the fourth book of the *Aeneid* of Vergil, is given in the prose version of J. W. Mackail. Dido has realized that Aeneas, drawn by his duty to reach the promised land, intends to desert her. Her grief and pride drive her to madness. Mercury, the messenger of the gods, warns Aeneas in a dream that, if he is to save his ships and his comrades, he must leave Carthage at dawn; for Dido will intend to destroy them.

Then indeed Aeneas, startled by the sudden phantom, leaps out of slumber and bestirs his crew to headlong haste. 'Awake, O men, and sit down to the thwarts; shake out sail speedily. A god sent from high heaven, lo! again spurs us to speed our flight and cut the twisted cables. We follow thee, holy one of heaven, whoso thou art, and again joyfully obey thy command. O be favourable; give gracious aid and bring fair sky and weather.' He spoke, and snatching his sword like lightning from the sheath, strikes at the hawser with the drawn steel. The same zeal catches all at once; rushing and tearing they quit the shore; the sea is hidden under their fleets; strongly they toss up the foam and sweep the blue water.

And now Dawn broke, and, leaving the saffron bed of Tithonus, shed her radiance anew over the world; when the Queen saw from her watch-tower the first light whitening, and the fleet standing out under squared sail, and discerned shore and haven empty of all their oarsmen. Thrice and four times she struck her hand on her lovely breast and rent her yellow hair: 'God!' she cries, 'shall he go? shall an alien make mock of our realm? Will they not issue in armed pursuit from all the city, and some launch ships from the dockyards? Go; bring fire in haste, serve out weapons, ply the oars! What do I talk? or where am I? what mad change is on my purpose? Alas, Dido! now evil deeds touch thee; that had been fitting once, when thou gavest away the crown. Behold the faith and hand of him, who, they say, carries his household's ancestral gods about with him! who stooped his shoulders to a father outworn with age! Could I not have riven his body in sunder and strewn it on the waves? and slain with the sword his comrades and his dear Ascanius, and served him from the banquet at his father's table? But the chance of battle had been dubious. If it had! whom did I fear in the death-agony? I should have borne fire-brands into his camp and filled his decks with flame, blotted out father and son and race together, and flung myself atop of all. Sun, whose fires lighten all the works of the world, and thou, Juno, mediatress and witness of these my distresses, and Hecate, cried on by night in crossways of cities, and you, fatal avenging sisters and gods of dying Elissa, hear me now; bend your just deity to my woes, and listen to our prayers. If it must needs be that the accursed one touch his haven and float up to land, if thus Jove's decrees demand, and this is the appointed term – yet, distressed in war by an armed and gallant nation, driven homeless from his borders, rent from Iulus' embrace, let him sue for succour and see death on death untimely on his people; nor when he has yielded him to the terms of a harsh peace, may he have joy of his kingdom or the pleasant light; but let him fall before his day and without burial amid its soil. This I pray; this and my blood with it I pour for the last utterance. Then do you, O Tyrians, pursue his seed with your hatred for all ages to come; send this guerdon to our ashes. Let no kindness nor truce be between the nations. Arise, some avenger, out of our dust, to follow the Dardanian settlers with fire-brand and steel. Now, then, whensoever strength shall be given, I invoke the enmity of shore to shore, wave to water, sword to sword; let their battles go down to their children's children.'

The second passage is taken from Tacitus' *Histories*. In it he sketches in advance the character of the age which he proposes to describe, A.D. 69–96. Perhaps Murphy's eighteenth-century translation gives some hint of Tacitus' terse and epigrammatic style, and of his enmity to the

Empire, which to him was the gods' visitation upon an erring Roman people.

The subject now before me presents a series of great events, and battles fierce and bloody; a portion of time big with intestine divisions, and even the intervals of peace deformed with cruelty and horror: the whole a tragic volume, displaying, in succession, four princes put to death; three civil wars; with foreign enemies a great number, and, in some conjunctures, both depending at once; prosperity in the East, disasters in the West; Illyricum thrown into convulsions; both the Gauls on the eve of a revolt; Britain conquered, and, in the moment of conquest, lost again; the Sarmatians and the Suevians leagued against the Romans; the Dacian name ennobled by alternate victory and defeat; and, finally, the Parthians taking the field under the banners of a pretended Nero. In the course of the work, we shall see Italy overwhelmed with calamities; new wounds inflicted, and the old, which time had closed, opened again and bleeding afresh; cities sacked by the enemy, or swallowed up by earthquakes, and the fertile country of Campania made a scene of desolation; Rome laid waste by fire; her ancient and most venerable temples smoking on the ground; the Capitol wrapt in flames by the hands of frantic citizens; the holy ceremonies of religion violated; adultery reigning without control; the adjacent islands filled with exiles; rocks and desert places stained with clandestine murder, and Rome itself a theatre of horror; where nobility of descent, and splendour of fortune, marked men out for destruction; where the vigour of mind that aimed at civil dignities, and the modesty that declined them, were offences without distinction; where virtue was a crime that led to certain ruin; where the guilt of informers, and the wages of their iniquity, were alike detestable; where the sacerdotal order, the consular dignity, the government of the provinces, and even the cabinet of the prince, were seized by that execrable race, as their lawful prey; where nothing was sacred, nothing safe from the hand of rapacity; where slaves were suborned, or, by their own malevolence, excited against their masters; where freedmen betrayed their patrons; and he, who had lived without an enemy, died by the treachery of a friend.

And yet this melancholy period, barren as it was of public virtue, produced some examples of truth and honour. Mothers went with their sons into voluntary exile; wives followed the fortunes of their husbands; relations stood forth in the cause of their unhappy kindred; sons appeared in defence of their fathers; slaves on the rack gave proofs of their fidelity; eminent citizens, under the hard hand of oppression, were reduced to want and misery, and, even in that distress, retained an unconquered spirit. We shall see others firm to the last, and, in their deaths, nothing inferior to the applauded characters of antiquity. In addition to the misfortunes usual in the course of human transactions, we shall see the earth teeming with prodigies, the sky overcast with omens, thunder rolling with dreadful denunciation, and a variety of prognostics, sometimes auspicious, often big with terror, occasionally uncertain, dark, equivocal, frequently direct and manifest. In a word, the gods never gave such terrible instructions, nor, by the slaughter of armies, made it so clear and evident, that, instead of extending protection to the Empire, it was their awful pleasure to let fall their vengeance on the crimes of an offending people.

The hurrying lightness of Horace's *Satires* can be seen in the following well-known passage, which describes how he was attacked while walking in Rome by a 'bore' who insisted on accompanying him. Juvenal's satires are more vitriolic, but are less easy to quote, for they are full of contemporary allusions. The version is by J. Conington.

> *Along the Sacred Road I strolled one day,*
> *Deep in some bagatelle (you know my way),*
> *When up comes one whose name I scarcely knew –*
> *'The dearest of dear fellows! how d'ye do?'*
> *He grasped my hand – 'Well, thanks: the same to you.'*
> *Then, as he still kept walking by my side,*
> *To cut things short, 'You've no commands?' I cried.*
> *'Nay, you should know me: I'm a man of lore.'*
> *'Sir, I'm your humble servant all the more.'*
> *All in a fret to make him let me go,*
> *I now walk fast, now loiter and walk slow,*
> *Now whisper to my servant, while the sweat*
> *Ran down so fast, my very feet were wet.*
> *'O had I but a temper worth the name,*
> *Like yours, Bolanus!' inly I exclaim,*
> *While he keeps running on at a hand-trot,*
> *About the town, the streets, I know not what.*

Finding I made no answer, 'Ah! I see,
You're at a strait to rid yourself of me;
But 'tis no use: I'm a tenacious friend,
And mean to hold you till your journey's end.'
'No need to take you such a round: I go
To visit an acquaintance you don't know:
Poor man! he's ailing at his lodging, far
Beyond the bridge, where Caesar's gardens are.'
'O, never mind: I've nothing else to do,
And want a walk, so I'll step on with you.'

Down go my ears, in donkey-fashion, straight;
You've seen them do it, when their load's too great.
'If I mistake not,' he begins, 'you'll find
Viscus not more, nor Varius, to your mind:
There's not a man can turn a verse so soon,
Or dance so nimbly when he hears a tune:
While, as for singing – ah! my forte is there:
Tigellius' self might envy me, I swear.'

He paused for breath: I falteringly strike in:
'Have you a mother? have you kith or kin
To whom your life is precious?' 'Not a soul:
My line's extinct: I have interred the whole.'
O happy they! (so into thought I fell)
After life's endless babble they sleep well:
My turn is next: dispatch me: for the weird
Has come to pass which I so long have feared,
The fatal weird a Sabine beldame sung,
All in my nursery days, when life was young:
'No sword nor poison e'er shall take him off,
Nor gout, nor pleurisy, nor racking cough:
A babbling tongue shall kill him: let him fly
All talkers, as he wishes not to die!'

Finally, we may quote the conclusion of the brilliant
biography of Agricola, Governor of Britain, by his son-in-
law, Tacitus. The translation is by H. Mattingly in the
Penguin Classics.

If there is any mansion for the spirits of the just, if, as the wise aver, great souls do not perish with the body, quiet, O Father, be your rest! May you call us, your household, from feeble regrets and unmanly mourning to contemplate your virtues, in presence of which sorrow and lamentation become a sin. May we honour you in better ways – by our admiration, by our undying praise, even, if our powers permit, by following your example. That is the true honour, the true affection of souls knit close to yours. To your daughter and widow I would suggest that they revere the memory of a father and a husband by continually pondering his deeds and sayings, and by cherishing his spiritual, above his physical, presence. Not that I would place an absolute ban on likenesses of marble or of bronze. But the image of the human face, like that face itself, is feeble and perishable, whereas the essence of the soul is eternal, never to be caught and expressed by the material and skill of a stranger, but only by you in your own living. All in Agricola that won our love and admiration abides and shall abide in the hearts of men, through endless ages, in the chronicles of fame. Many of the great men of old will be drowned in oblivion, their name and fame forgotten. Agricola's story has been told to posterity and by that he will live.

CHAPTER VI

THE ROMAN PRACTICAL GENIUS

The best preferred doing to talking.   SALLUST

Only those, if there are any, who are outside your Empire are to be pitied for the blessings which they are denied. Better than all others you have demonstrated the universal saying, that the earth is the mother of all and the common fatherland of all. Greek and barbarian, with his property or without it, can go with ease wherever he likes, just as though going from one homeland to another. The Cilician Gates hold no terror, nor the narrow and desert approaches from Arabia to Egypt, nor inaccessible mountains nor uncrossed expanses of rivers, nor tribes inhospitable to the stranger: for safety it is enough to be a Roman or rather one of your subjects. In very deed you have made real Homer's dictum that the earth is the property of all: you have measured the whole world, spanned rivers with bridges of divers kinds, cut through mountains to make level roads for traffic, filled desolate places with farmsteads and made life easier by supplying its necessities amid law and order.

Everywhere are gymnasia, fountains, gateways, temples, factories, schools, and it could be said in technical phrase that the world which from the beginning has been labouring in illness has now been put in the way of health. ... Cities are radiant in their splendour and their grace, and the whole earth is as trim as a garden.

AELIUS ARISTIDES (2ND CENTURY, A.D.)

SOMETHING was said in an earlier chapter about Roman pleasures; and it was suggested that there was an element of grossness in them. But the typically Roman source of satisfaction was really derived from the nature of his genius, which was in all things essentially practical. In the practical management of men and things the Roman displayed his specific character and took peculiar pleasure. Of his management of men we have already seen something in the growth and organization of the Empire; a word must now be said about his management of things.

The Roman loved his country, and he loved to possess land and to take up the challenge which it offered. He took from it the joy of ownership and the satisfaction of making it produce. The following poem by Claudian, though written when the Empire was drawing to its end, will express the feeling which runs through Latin literature. The translation is by F. Fawkes.

Blest who, content with what the country yields,
Lives in his own hereditary fields;
Who can with pleasure his past life behold,
Whose roof paternal saw him young and old;
And as he tells his long adventures o'er,
A stick supports him where he crawled before;
Who ne'er was tempted from his farm to fly,
And drink new streams beneath a foreign sky:
No merchant he, solicitous of gain,
Dreads not the storms that lash the sounding main:
Nor soldier, fears the summons to the war,
Nor the hoarse clamours of the noisy bar.
Unskilled in business, to the world unknown,
He ne'er beheld the next contiguous town.
Yet nobler objects to his view are given,
Fair flowery fields and star-embellished heaven.
He marks no change of consuls, but computes
Alternate consuls by alternate fruits;
Maturing autumns store of apples bring,
And flowerets are the luxury of spring.
His farm that catches first the sun's bright ray
Sees the last lustre of his beams decay:
The passing hours erected columns show,
And are his landmarks and his dials too.
Yon spreading oak a little twig he knew,
And the whole grove in his remembrance grew.
Verona's walls remote as India seem,
Benacus is th' Arabian Gulf to him.

Yet health three ages lengthens out his span,
And grandsons hail the vigorous old man.
Let others vainly sail from shore to shore —
Their joys are fewer and their labours more.

Admittedly, if every Roman had acted literally on this ideal, there would have been no Roman Empire. None the less, the love of the land exercised a strong pull. The discharged soldier clamoured for his smallholding; Horace's affection for his modest farm is sincere. The rich bought their country houses not purely from motives of investment or display or escape from the bustle of town. The poet who truly expresses the Italian's love of the land — a love which willingly recognizes no less the invincible thraldom of labour imposed by the land itself than the rewards and pleasures of labour — was Vergil, who wrote his *Georgics* at the beginning of the Empire. In the second *Georgics* there is a celebrated passage in praise of the country. How happy is the husbandman — if only he knew his blessings. Not for him the ceremony and social formalities of the town, the luxury of fine buildings and elaborate furniture, but peace and honest simplicity and the freedom which the open country gives, and the sounds of the fields, and the beasts of the farm and of the wild, and simple rustic religion and reverence given to the aged, and to the last relics of righteousness before she fled from earth. Vergil's first wish is to learn of Nature's laws and their working, of the sun and stars and tides; and, if he cannot master them, his second wish is to live with Nature, with streams and woods and the gods of the countryside, heedless of politics and empire and kingdoms that rise and fall, undisturbed by the wrangles of the law-courts and the struggles of ambition and the applause of the mob or the exile which awaits him who fails. It is the soil which offers a worthy livelihood, which sustains son and grandson, and gives increase of crop and beast and vine; here is real family life, and traditions of goodness, and innocent gaiety. This was the manner of life in which were bred the Romans of old, and through it Rome was made the most glorious thing in the world.

And in the same poem is another equally celebrated passage in which Vergil praises Italy. With Italy neither the wealth of Persia, nor of Arabia, nor of any Eastern country can contend. True, she has not the mythical glories of a remote past; but her crops are heavy, her vines and olives are laden, her flocks multiply; here is perpetual spring and a twice-yearly harvest, and harmful beasts and plants are unknown. And then the real Roman breaks out in Vergil. However much the Roman loved the country – and it was seldom not in his mind – it was in the city that he saw the distinctive mark of civilization and the specific work of Rome in the world.

Think, too [the passage continues] of all those noble cities, the work of men's hands, towns toilfully piled on steep-cut rocks, with rivers gliding beneath their immemorial walls. Think of the seas which wash the land on either side, and of the lakes, the great Lago di Como, and the Lago di Garda which heaves with the roaring swell of an ocean – the harbours, and the Lucrine haven with its strengthening mole and the sea noisily chafing against it ... It was this land that bred a tough race of men, the Marsi, the Sabellian youth, the Ligurian endured to hardship, the Volscian armed with his short spear; that bred men like the Decii, like Marius and the great Camillus, and the Scipiones hardened in war, and thou, too, great Caesar [Augustus], who now triumphant on the furthest shores of Asia dost repel the unwarlike Indian from the embattled hills of Rome.

Then comes the conclusion of the whole matter: Rome was great in her land, and great in her sons; and Vergil's task is to sing in the towns built by those sons a Roman

song glorifying labour in Italian fields – as once Hesiod
had sung to the Greeks.

Hail to thee, great mother of harvests, land of Saturn, great
mother of men; in thy honour I essay to tell of the things of that
art of husbandry which from ancient times has been thy glory; I
dare to unseal those sacred springs, and through Roman towns I
sing the song which Hesiod sang to the Greeks.

The Roman regarded the organic life of the town as the
chief instrument of civilization; but he did not forget the
country – its pleasures, its challenge to work and management, its essential role as the mother of a nation's sons.

In the multiplication of towns throughout the Empire
Rome was singularly direct and practical in her methods.
In most of her provinces town-life already existed : it was
further encouraged and the towns were often replanned
and rebuilt. In Britain there were no towns before the
Romans came; the only collections of dwellings were
placed upon high ground and they were made for defen-
sive purposes against neighbouring tribes. For a century
or two town life in the valleys was deliberately created
as a means of spreading a Roman manner of life. But the
Briton did not take to it; the towns decayed; they were
deserted because the people preferred to make their livelihood in the woods and open lands rather than to act as
middlemen or as artisans for the surrounding country.
Roman civilization, of a very diluted character, betook
itself to large self-supporting 'villas' or country houses.
The policy of creating towns failed in Britain as it did not
fail on the Continent.

Whenever the Romans founded a town, it was planned
upon very definite lines. By means of a simple piece of
apparatus by which the surveyor determined a right
angle, two wide streets were drawn intersecting at ninety

degrees. From this cross-roads as a starting-point rect-
angular plots of land were marked; at regular intervals
streets of specified width were laid out. We hear of the
'building line', and of rules about the height of buildings
and of regulations excluding heavy traffic during specified
hours. At the centre were public buildings, offices, the
basilica or public hall used for meetings and law-courts,
sometimes a library, always a temple, and the open square
of the forum with colonnades. Shops were often assigned
to particular quarters, with trades of like character con-
gregating together. Monumental arches at the entrances
of the town carried sculptures and statues, and sometimes
four-way arches covered the junction of two roads. Baths
and theatres and amphitheatres were a necessity even in
small towns.

Into the towns was brought a plentiful supply of water
carried in underground channels or on aqueducts; from
storage tanks it might be carried in lead pipes into houses.
Fourteen aqueducts, of a total length of 265 miles, met
the needs of the city of Rome, delivering perhaps fifty
gallons each day per head of the population. In many
regions of the provinces the water-supply was better in
Roman times than today; and some of the Roman aqueducts are still in use. The well-known Pont du Gard near
Nîmes carries across the valley of the Gard the water
which up to that point is enclosed in subterranean channels; it is composed of three tiers of arches one above
another, and its greatest height is 160 feet. The aqueduct,
still standing, which supplied Carthage was 95 miles in
length, partly tunnelled, partly carried on gigantic arches;
that at Tarragona in Spain was 22 miles, and at Lyon
11 miles. Low-pressure pipes were used: high pressure
implies cast-iron pipes which the Romans could not
make. Water power was used for milling and sawing, and

fountains in public squares and gardens and street corners caught the sunlight and brought a sense of refreshment to dusty towns. The maintenance of aqueducts was a public service carried out by state or municipal servants.

The same massive grandeur is a mark of everything which the Romans constructed; they built for use and for permanence. Roman roads are the supreme example. Originally their purpose was military and administrative; they grew according to need, and in time they served every need of war and peace, trade and communication. The Roman surveyor preferred straight lines, plotted from ridge to ridge; but he was guided by the lie of the country, by considerations of gradient and military defence. He built a zigzag road through mountainous districts, the Apennines and the Alps, with superb engineering skill, but across a plain he took the shortest route, ignoring existing tracks. Round the country of Cumae and Naples long tunnels were cut in the hard deposits of volcanic rock. The surface of roads was elaborately laid with strata of different materials, and the foundations have lasted till today. Equally elaborate and permanent were many of the drains and sewers.

The Roman methods of building houses, temples, halls, baths, theatres, bridges, harbours, and the like cannot here detain us, for a separate volume is necessary to do them justice. But it should be noticed that perhaps the great achievement of Roman architects was the spanning of a great area by means of vaulting. A skeleton vault of brick was first constructed and concrete was poured in between the ribs. When the concrete set, the brick ribs showed from below; and, since the vast roof exerted no lateral thrust, buttresses supporting the walls were unnecessary. This method was a Roman invention. Other features of Roman architecture are more questionable;

marble was applied to walls and pillars in thin slabs like veneer, and ornament tended to be applied unintelligently, with no relation to structural function. In sculpture, ornamentation, carving, and painting the Romans were dependent on the Greek and Syrian artists and craftsmen and had little taste of their own, though the method of presenting themes, especially those of political or religious significance, was largely influenced by the Romans themselves. Indeed, whereas some years ago it was supposed that the Romans had no interest in art and never developed a style or technique of their own, modern study finds in Roman sculptures and architecture an individuality and character not to be despised. In particular they took great interest in portraiture, and some of the Roman busts and bas-reliefs are remarkable for their realism and careful representation of character.

Practical management and construction on a grand scale appealed to the Roman. Did he ever invent anything? Very little, but none the less he played a very important role, which must be explained at some length.

While the Romans were securing their position in Italy and acquiring their Mediterranean Empire, schools of learning flourished in several cities of the East, notably Alexandria and Pergamum. Here flourished what is often called 'later Greek' science, but it must be understood that many of its most famous exponents were Hellenized Asiatics. Notable work was done in mathematics, mechanics, astronomy, medicine, botany; these studies were pursued somewhat in isolation, and there was no attempt to make a systematic philosophy of science. One of the earliest mathematicians was Euclid, whose work was more extensive than the *Elements of Geometry*: for he was interested in optics and music and originated the investigation into the idea of 'limits', which was the germ of the calculus. Aristarchus (of Samos) attempted to measure the distance of the sun and moon from the earth and to compute their relative sizes, and he believed the earth to revolve round the sun. Archimedes of Syracuse (287–212 B.C.), one of the greatest mathematicians who have lived, is familiar to us; to him are due the discovery of 'specific gravity', the Archimedean screw, the theory of levers, the evaluation of π, but his works covered vast tracts of mechanics and hydrostatics and geometry; and he invented engines of war to defend Syracuse against the Romans. Hero of Alexandria (?100 B.C.) was equally catholic in his pursuits, though not comparable with Archimedes in genius: mechanics, optics, hydraulics, cogwheels and pulleys, the worm drive, the refraction of light and a primitive theodolite based on it, architects' and builders' devices are among the subjects of which he treats. In geography great progress was made; Eratosthenes of Cyprus (about 230 B.C.) laid the foundation of mathematical geography, measuring the earth, plotting parallels, suggesting the navigation of the globe; Strabo (of Amasia in Pontus, born 63 B.C.) wrote a general geography, drawing maps which realized the importance of projection. But it was Ptolemy of Alexandria (died about A.D. 180) who wrote the most complete geography that we have. And so the story might be prolonged – Dioscorides (about A.D. 55) wrote about drugs and the plants from which they are made, and the influence of his treatise can be seen in every pharmacopoeia today; similarly, the works of Galen of Pergamum (A.D. 131–201), of which twenty-one volumes survive, contain a stupendous treatment of biology and medicine: translated into Latin and Syrian and Arabic they dominated thought and practice in these fields throughout the Middle Ages, and for a thousand years practically no new work was done.

Discovery of this kind was taking place within the Roman world. It has sometimes been suggested that the Romans failed completely to take advantage of the discoveries of the Greeks, and that this failure was due to lack of imagination or of brains or of interest. Now this is scarcely quite fair to the Romans : several considerations must be borne in mind. The inventors themselves did not carry their discoveries very far and failed to make the practical applications. Archimedes himself stooped to elaborate engines of war only at the urgent insistence of the King of Syracuse ; for, we are told, he held mechanical work and practical skills to be sordid and unworthy. His passion lay in the quest of beautiful and subtle theory which was uncontaminated by the ordinary needs of life. Euclid replied to a questioner who asked what was the good of geometry by asking the bystander to give him a penny if he felt he had to make gain from his study of geometry. Moreover, when practical applications were in fact made, they were often trivial. Hero's researches are by no means to be despised, but he gives page after page to the description of devices which are, it is true, amusing, but which embody ideas capable of more useful and serious development. For instance, the expansion of the hot air within a hollow altar works a mechanism to open the doors of the temple without human agency ; the propulsion of air caused by water falling from one tank into another causes metal birds placed on the edge of a fountain to whistle, whereat an owl turns on its perch to eye them disapprovingly; steam led into a hollow sphere furnished with right-angled jets makes the sphere revolve – the principle of jet propulsion in its simplest form. But the principles were taken little further; for the most part the demonstrations remained on the laboratory bench: they were not carried further into industry.

Secondly, a good deal of the work of these 'scientists' was carried out amid circumstances which the Romans had created. For example, Strabo, the geographer, was able to travel only because the Roman peace gave the opportunity and because officials lent their aid. He worked in Rome and came into contact with provincial administrators and generals and merchants and was able to put together masses of authentic information. Dioscorides who wrote on drugs was an army surgeon. Galen worked in Rome where he had a large practice, a colossal reputation, and three Emperors as his patients. Ptolemy used the itineraries furnished to him by Roman officials, traders, and soldiers. In some of the results of this activity the Romans were interested, and they made the practical applications which were most obvious. The Greeks might engage in the professions of medicine, architecture, surgery, and the like; it was the Romans who built hospitals and organized an army medical service, or used geometry for the work of road-building or the conveying of water.

Thirdly, the Romans are justly regarded as a practical people. Though they may have relied upon non-Roman technicians, the direction of policy lay with them, and they reserved for themselves the work of management. What they really enjoyed was the management of land, or the subjugation of intractable nature; they applied all practicable means for turning deserts into inhabited and cultivated lands, for organizing resources and spreading amenities and raising standards of life. In all this there was creative imagination no less than in theoretical discovery.

Fourthly, it must be remembered that the Romans were faced with the task of spreading existing knowledge rather than with enlarging it; they had taken on the work of civilizing the West, and existing knowledge was enough for the peoples whom they were educating – indeed, more than enough, as those peoples became increasingly mixed with barbarians penetrating into the Western provinces.

Again, economic conditions did not demand new techniques and inventions. Though slave labour was less abundant in the second century of the Empire than earlier, there was no dearth of labour, and there was little incentive to think out methods which would economize time or toil. Moreover, the economic tendencies of the Empire were all against the development of new processes. Though manufactured articles were exported from one province to another, or from Italy to the provinces, they were not exported on any scale comparable with present practice; and, as the provinces built up their own industries, they tended to satisfy their own needs and to look no further afield for markets. In the third century there was a movement of population away from the towns, for reasons which we shall see in a later chapter; and, as country estates grew larger and were increasingly managed under an almost feudal system, old methods of manufacture became stereotyped and were sufficient to supply the needs of a limited area. Districts lived on their own economy, and were independent of the resources or manufactures of neighbouring districts. When self-sufficiency of this kind prevails, no stimulus is offered to the invention of new techniques.

Finally, there is no doubt that the Roman tended to dislike the routine and the actual manual labour of industry. The point of view of the well-to-do Roman is put clearly in a letter of Seneca, and it should be observed that in essence it is little different from the attitude of Plato. Seneca derives from Poseidonius, the last of the Greek philosophers in the direct line of Plato and Aristotle, a classification of arts into (i) the common and debasing,

(ii) those which amuse the senses of sight and hearing by illusionist tricks, (iii) those suitable to the early education of children, (iv) the liberal, or, as they should be called, the arts consistent with freedom (*liberae*). The first are 'manual arts', engaged solely in supplying the needs of life; the second are dexterous enough, but concerned only with a rather cheap amusement; the third are the skills acquired in education; they are akin to liberal arts, for they are introductory to them. It is only the liberal arts which put a man in the way of virtue, though they cannot make him virtuous: 'Only those arts are liberal which are concerned with virtue', that is, with human character and the human spirit manifesting itself in moral behaviour. And in the last resort it is philosophy alone which deals with good and evil. Two or three generations earlier Cicero had said much the same kind of thing in a long discussion given in the first book of his treatise *On Duties*. He thinks there can be nothing in a workshop worthy of a free man; the occupations 'which the public detests', as for example those of customs officers and money-lenders, are 'sordid'; retail trade, since it buys to sell immediately, is not honourable; to undertake imports on a large scale and so to satisfy the needs of a large area is more respectable. Arts which pander to pleasure are despicable; medicine, architecture, and the like are higher in the scale since they involve long views and their utility is obvious. There is something sordid about all gain: only for agriculture is high praise reserved, 'nothing better, nothing more attractive, nothing more suitable for a free man'. The highest occupation is, of course, public service, undertaken with the equipment of the virtues of integrity and devotion, of kindliness and loyalty to the good of all fellow-citizens. In spite of these views, men like Cicero and Seneca were in fact concerned with commercial undertakings, but only, as it were, at long range and on a large scale. And in the course of the Empire these old-fashioned prejudices were much modified : men tended to agree with Vespasian's dictum, that money does not smell. But it was too late and too difficult to change a tradition; besides, the other influences which we have indicated above were all against the development of new techniques, and such influences as these are often beyond the diagnosis, or even the understanding, of the men of the day, who certainly are powerless to counteract them.

CHAPTER VII

THE ROMAN ATTITUDE TO RELIGION
AND PHILOSOPHY

Cicero ... of supreme eloquence and of the most perfect watchfulness in weighing and measuring his words ... by whom philosophy in the Latin tongue was begun and was brought to perfection.

ST AUGUSTINE

IN earlier chapters we have seen the attitude of the Roman to his own religion. He tended to think of religion in terms of history, and history was the history of Rome. For the individual there was little of personal appeal; he had the feeling that somehow he was incorporated into a state which in some incomprehensible way had relations with the divine powers which were behind its history and destiny; moreover, it was desirable that he should keep on the right side of the many gods who formed the spiritual background against which his own life was enacted, and that he should put himself in the line of their activities or purposes. In the legends of Roman heroes he had examples of certain moral qualities which acquired a sanction more than human because they were set in a context of history which was under divine care. But of emotional appeal, of spiritual strengthening, of explanation of life and its immediate problems, Roman religion had little to offer. The Roman either stood firm and unshaken upon a narrow basis of right and duty – a 'mind conscious of the right' – and refused to stray into things which were beyond the power of man to comprehend; or he supplied the deficiencies of his Roman religion from elsewhere – from alien religions or from philosophy.

The attitude of the Romans to foreign religion can be
shortly described. When the official curators of the state
religion admitted into public recognition a non-Roman
cult by granting it a place among public festivals or a site
for a temple, they saw to it that the cult was transformed
in a way suitable to Roman tradition. The legend or story
often underwent changes, the ritual and terminology were
modified, and the cult bore a strong Roman imprint.
When this was not possible, at least the objectionable
elements were purged out of it.

In the last century of the Republic the state religion
lost some of its hold upon Roman sentiment. The increase
of wealth and power had led to a materialism which in
its first flush could do without the gods; the expansion of
the Empire and the flow of foreigners to Rome in the
processes of trade and commerce, and of other activities in
which Rome was now plunged, had brought foreign cults
to Italy. These were readily embraced; for they offered
an emotional element lacking in Roman religion and they
exalted the importance of the individual, offering excitement and personal experience and often a destiny in a
world to come. Moreover, the contrast between the
'people' and the older and governing elements of the
population of Rome was now very marked; the people
were enlarged by foreigners who were of a temperament
different from the Roman and politically were opposed
to the senatorial party. From natural inclination and for
political and social reasons they were indifferent or hostile
to the religion and standards of the older Roman tradition,
and found greater excitement in newer forms of cult.
Pressure was too great, and of necessity the state tolerated
all religions as practised by individuals provided that they
were not immoral, or politically dangerous in the sense
that they preached political doctrine under the form of

religion. By degrees several Eastern cults received official recognition, though caution as to their number and character was always exercised and their temples were refused a place within the sacred boundary of the city of Rome.

For example, in the Second Punic War a Sibylline oracle commanded that the Romans should welcome Cybele, the 'great Mother', of Mount Ida in Asia Minor, if they would be saved from Hannibal. The goddess was escorted into Italy, into Rome, housed in the Temple of Victory with her Oriental priests and wild music – and deliberately neglected. Citizens were forbidden to take part in the ritual appropriate to her as a 'Nature' goddess, and the exotic ceremonies and the strange orientalism of her priests became objects of ridicule. Romanized festivals were kept in her honour, but it was only in the third century A.D., when the Roman capital accepted more freely Oriental influences, that the cult reached full expression. From its introduction in 204 B.C. it was under the control of the commission of fifteen charged with the superintendence of public worship. Again, in 186 B.C. thousands of the people of Rome were seized by the frenzies incidental to the worship of Bacchus, newly introduced into Rome. Public order and public decency were threatened. The cult was suppressed by law. But, if any citizen felt it a matter of necessity and conscience to pursue this worship, he could obtain leave from the city magistrate (who must consult the Senate), and not more than five worshippers must meet together. In the same way astrologers, proselytizing Jews, and magicians and many others were ejected at various times in the last century of the Republic and the beginning of the Empire. It was not till the third century A.D. that Oriental gods, Egyptian or Syrian or Persian, found their way within

the sacred city boundary; so firmly had Augustus restored
the Roman cults, and so seriously did the senatorial circles,
to whom he had restored the custodianship of Roman
religion, take their duties.

The tests applied to foreign cults, therefore, were three:
(i) Would they upset the dominant position of the Roman
cults? (ii) Were they politically unsafe? (iii) Were they
morally undesirable? If these tests were satisfied, toleration was complete.

From the time of Augustus a new form of Roman cult
makes its appearance – the worship of the Emperor. The
phrase 'the worship of the Roman Emperor' is here deliberately used, because it is commonly used; whether it
is the best phrase is open to doubt, as the following brief
account may perhaps suggest. At the risk of over-simplifi-
cation we may approach it from three angles: first, from
the viewpoint of the Eastern provinces; secondly, from
Rome; thirdly, from the Western provinces.

In the Eastern Mediterranean the cult of the Emperor
was a spontaneous growth. The line between God and
man was indistinctly drawn. The theory that the gods and
heroes of old were men who had served well their country
or mankind was commonly accepted; philosophy had
spoken of the divine spark or element in man. Homage
had been paid in Oriental fashion to the successors of
Alexander in forms and language borrowed from religion.
A ruler who had conferred benefits upon his subjects was
saluted by titles such as 'Benefactor' (*Euergetes*) and
'Saviour' (*Soter*). The question of kingship and its responsibilities received much attention in more than one school
of Greek philosophy, and an extensive literature – some
of which survives – discussed the qualities of the ideal
king; the justification for his office was found in such
qualities as love of humanity, justice, kindliness, and ser-

vice to his subjects. For the divinity of rulers resided in
the degree to which they manifested the highest principles
of divine character. In the good ruler godhead was revealed in such form as it could be on the human level.
Eastern peoples so readily attached seemingly divine titles
to rulers that Roman governors of provinces in Asia Minor
frequently received them. There is nothing surprising,
therefore, in their eagerness to salute with extravagant
titles the Emperor who had given them peace and prosperity.

In Rome and Italy matters were different. The idea
of ascribing divinity, in any sense, to a living man was
repugnant. But, as we have seen, the attitude of the
Romans to their past was such that they did venerate
the memory of their great men, and they personified the
destiny of Rome and the moral qualities which had made
her great. Moreover, the idea of the 'genius' (see page 19)
expressed in sober form something of the feeling which
the Eastern Mediterranean expressed less restrainedly.
And so the birthday of Augustus was celebrated as an
event of unique importance to Rome; he or his office was
associated with Rome, and a cult of 'Rome and Augustus'
was officially authorized and encouraged as a declaration
of loyalty. The name Augustus – which was a title and
not a proper name – called up ideas of 'increase' (cf.
English 'augment') and 'sanctity'. This cult was immediately popular throughout Italy and in every township;
it was organized by 'colleges' and 'sodalities' and practised
with enthusiasm. But no Emperor received 'consecration'
during his lifetime, and not every Emperor upon his death.

In the Western provinces the imperial cult was celebrated in municipalities and at the places where the
provincial councils met. Of the elements of which it was
composed – Rome and Augustus – the emphasis fell upon

Rome; for it was Roman civilization which they admired. Civilization was new to them in a way in which it was not new to the East; the cult summed up for them the blessings of law and order, trade and letters, material prosperity and a safe frontier defence against the threats from the northern barbarians.

After the end of the second century, when an Emperor might be an African or a Syrian or a Thracian, the cult took on a different form in Italy, and flattery and sycophancy tolerated whatever extravagances an Emperor might demand. When the god Jupiter could become identified with the Persian Sun-god, similar orientalizing changes might be expected in the imperial cult. The whole family of the reigning Emperor might be 'deified'; but this meant little more than the observance of certain outward forms and the granting of a certain sacrosanctity.

We must see in the cult an expression of loyalty to the Principate, to the government of Rome, and to the ideas for which Rome stood. To the role of Emperor were attached certain 'virtues', such as we have already seen associated with the ruler in Hellenistic philosophy. 'Virtue', kindness, justice, and a religious sense of duty are taken for granted; legends on coins and inscriptions show many more, as, for example, *providentia*, the care for the future welfare of the Empire. Not that the association of these virtues with the Emperor necessarily meant that they were displayed by the reigning Emperor, though signal acts of generosity or measures of statesmanship were often so attested; ascriptions of such virtues indicated rather the general ideal of the imperial function.

The world was full of religions and philosophies; the ease of movement, the manifold needs of trade and army service and official duties and the like sent men of every class travelling on a diversity of errands from one end of

the Empire to another. They took their religions with
them. The worship of Mithras, the Persian Sun-god, is to
be found wherever Roman troops were stationed and
upon the lines of communication; for he was especially a
soldiers' god. Silvanus was a primitive god of the Italian
countryside. Yet Silvanus is sometimes described as
invictus, 'unconquered', an epithet of Mithras; that is
to say, one god is identified or fused with another. We can
trace the movements of gods by means of the inscriptions
on altars, votive offerings, tablets of dedication, and
records of thanks which have been unearthed. Jupiter of
the Capitol is found in the East, Egyptian gods in the
Western provinces; and the ritual of one cult borrowed
freely from that of another. Often numerous gods were
invoked in one long formula – a typical dedication is to
'Jupiter Optimus Maximus, Juno Regina, Minerva
Sancta, the Sun Mithras, Hercules, Mars, Mercury, the
genius of the place, and all gods and goddesses'. The
fusion of gods and cults was brought about by bewilder-
ment at the large number of available cults, by obvious
affinities in ritual and in promises to their devotees, and
by an earnest desire to make certain of divine favour.
These causes and motives all helped to bring about a
monotheistic outlook; and this tendency was reinforced by
such notions as reached the populace from the teachings
of philosophers.

From religion we pass to philosophy, and as a bridge
to make that passage we use Lucretius, a poet of powerful
and original genius, whose passion it was to discredit
religion and whose achievement to display perhaps the
most sincere religious enthusiasm in the whole of Roman
literature. We know practically nothing about Lucretius;
in 55 B.C. he died in middle age leaving his poem un-
finished. In it he set out to interpret the world and human

life and conduct in the light of the philosophy of Epicurus, a Greek philosopher (died *c*. 270 B.C.). And he succeeded, for, though *On the Nature of Things* is a didactic poem of six books expounding in the most technical language of the day a philosophic, or as we should say now a scientific, view of the world, no rationalist street-corner orator could exhibit greater ardour, no nature-mystic more penetrating feeling for the mysterious and majestic workings of material nature. For Lucretius was afire with the hopes excited by his prophet, Epicurus :

When before the eyes of men Human Life lay still upon the ground, prostrate in foul dejection, crushed and burdened with the dead weight of Religion, which put forth her head from the heavenly places and with the terror of her countenance lowered upon mortal men and brooded over them – then it was that a man of Greece first had the courage to lift up his eyes – the eyes of a mortal – to meet her eyes and to be the first to withstand her to the face. This man neither stories about the gods nor the gods' lightnings nor heaven with its threats and its thunder could keep within bounds: they only spurred the more his mind's searching courage to long to be the first to splinter the bars that lock the gates of Nature's world. Therefore his mind's violent energy carried through to victory; he passed far beyond the flaming ramparts of the universe and ranged in mind and spirit through the un-measured whole. Thence bringing his spoils in triumph he comes back to tell us what things can come into being, what things can-not – in short, what is the principle by which each thing's poten-tialities are marked out, its boundary stone set deep down within itself. That is how in her turn Religion is overthrown and trampled down underfoot; this man's victory puts us on a level with heaven.

Such is Lucretius' debt to Epicurus. Briefly, Epicure-anism was derived from the atomic determinism of Democritus. The universe is the result of chance agglomerations of atoms, which vary in size and shape and fall through space. As they fall, they are liable to swerve – why is not clear – and to collide and to form combinations, and so the world has variety, and law is not rigid, and man is subject to predetermining causes over which he has no control. All things are made of matter, even the soul, though matter varies in degree of 'thinness'; matter can come apart into atoms, which alone are indestructible; therefore all may perish except atoms and the bodies of the gods which reside in the empty spaces between the universes and so can collide with nothing and so are immortal. If everything is material, ideas and impressions of the senses – sight, for example – are material; they arise because things throw off husks of atoms, as it were, which strike the sense organs of the mind itself. Thus, the gods really exist, for we have an idea of them; they are happy and care nothing for the happiness of man, whom they did not even create. Man may revere the gods and expose himself to their emanations and so perhaps gain something of their qualities; contemplation, therefore, may confer some benefits. But the gods do not willingly or consciously influence men. Man's goal is happiness – not over-indulgence in pleasure, for this may bring pain; calm of body and of mind is the aim. Above all, get rid of fears, fear of death and the displeasure of the gods; death is unconsciousness; the displeasure of the gods is a myth.

And so the poem expounds the implication of this doctrine for human knowledge and human life, and ranges far and wide. Here are the topics of the fifth book: the nature of the world and mortality; the formation of the world; the motions of the heavenly bodies; vegetation and animals and their origin; the extinction of animals in the struggle for existence; primitive man; early civilization; origin of speech; discovery of fire; beginnings of political life and of religion; discovery of metals; early war; invention of music; civilization as a whole. The scientific theory is developed with an ingenuity and a conviction which carry us along; it is nothing if not thorough. For example, seventeen reasons are given why the soul must perish with the body, and the conclusion of the matter begins thus:

Death therefore to us is nothing, and concerns us not one whit, since the nature of the mind is proved to be mortal. Just as we ourselves felt no pain in days now past, when the Carthaginians gathered against us from all sides to engage in battle and all things were shaken in war's fearful confusion and trembled in terror beneath the high confines of the heavens, when men wondered which of the two nations it would be to whose empire all human kind by sea and by land would fall – so too in the days to come when we shall be no more, when the body and the soul, from whose union we are fused into single beings, are put asunder, then beyond cavil to us who shall be no more nothing at all can happen, nothing can arouse sensation, no, not even if the earth be confounded with the sea and the sea with the heavens.

But the passages which compel the utmost admiration are those in which imaginative insight describes the workings of nature, and the life of man in his earliest days. Lucretius had little in the way of anthropological data, no tribes to observe at first hand, no collection of fossils or implements, no cave-drawings. Yet his pictures are astonishingly vivid and, judged by modern theories, correct. Again, his observation of nature is careful of detail and searching and sympathetic; his delineation of types of human character and emotion and motive is sure and convincing. In such passages as these the Latin hexameter verse rose to new heights and was not surpassed.

The poem stands remote and unique. Epicureanism had no great following in Rome; Vergil and Horace played with it and gave it up. Lucretius had no sectaries to whom to preach, no predecessors to show him the way, no posterity of readers to admire him as a philosopher; he was merely a poet whose genius bent to its will a most intractable theme. With all his passionate materialism Lucretius protests not so much against religion as against the forms of religion which were gaining influence in Rome. He has been accused of exaggerating the religious crudity against which he inveighs – reliance on dreams, and magical rites, and sacrifices, and charms, and rank superstition. Did Lucretius exaggerate their place in Roman religion? Certainly, if he had thought only of Roman religion; but he thought also, and probably first, of those Eastern practices which in his time were securing a firmer hold upon Roman sentiment. It was not the gods, nor indeed an outlook upon life which admitted its marvels and mystery, against which Lucretius protested: what drove him almost to madness was man's self-inflicted and degrading enslavement to crude and terrifying superstitions which a few moments of clear reasoning would dissipate into nothingness. 'The life of fools in the end becomes a hell upon earth.' With the breathless fervour of a religious convert he attacked in the name of reason the irreligion of religion.

If Epicureanism had not a great following at Rome, the reverse is true of Stoicism, for the Romans were natural Stoics long before they heard of Stoicism. The founder of Stoicism was Zeno (350–260 B.C.) of Citium, who lived and taught at Athens. Stoicism looked back upon the field of Greek philosophy and was in contact with philosophical ideas which emanated from the East. Its adherents engaged with most of the problems hitherto raised by philosophical speculation – metaphysical, physical, psychological, ethical, logical, political – and they spread their teaching far and wide over the Eastern Mediterranean. But Roman Stoicism was very different.

No Roman adopted the whole of any philosophy; some parts did not interest him, other parts he adapted to his own instinctive beliefs and found in them a statement of what he had never clearly articulated for himself. It may be perhaps an exaggeration to say that the Roman adopted only what suited his Roman ideals, for undoubtedly philosophical studies did influence the conduct and outlook of many. But certainly the Roman was not greatly interested in the coherence of a system, or in pursuing the fundamental questions of metaphysics. He was interested primarily in action and its springs and justification. Hence Roman philosophy is largely eclectic, and it is concerned chiefly with morals.

We hear that in 155 B.C. Athens sent an embassy to Rome and that it included the leading exponent of each of the three schools of philosophy, the Stoic, the Peripatetic (successors of Aristotle), the Academic (successors of Plato). Enormous audiences listened. Very soon afterwards Panaetius of Rhodes (died about 109 B.C.) visited Rome, and became a close friend of Scipio Aemilianus and of his literary friends, Polybius and the rest. Panaetius himself greatly modified Stoic doctrine, doubtless to suit the Roman character. Later still Poseidonius taught in Rhodes; Cicero visited him there in 78 B.C. and clearly was greatly in his debt.

Estimates of Cicero as a philosophical writer have varied. Certainly his influence on European thought and letters has been profound, at some epochs greater than that of Plato or Aristotle. At the present moment he is derided as a mere middleman of no great intelligence. In modest depreciation of his philosophical works he once wrote in a letter to Atticus, 'they are copies and therefore cost less trouble; I supply only the words, and I don't lack those!', and he is now taken at his word. In one sense he was right, but in supplying the words he rendered an incalculable service to European thought and letters. He moulded the Latin language into such form that it became supple enough and clear enough to put within the reach of any intelligent man not only the philosophical ideas with which his age was familiár, but also those ideas which were yet to be created by Christian thought and controversy and by European science and learning in every field. Moreover, even if Cicero's works are derivative, they select what they derive and present it in such form that there is probably no better introduction to moral philosophy – not excepting Plato himself. Of originality there is none – except in style, language, and presentation; but century after century learned its philosophical grammar from these works and they are still invaluable. Here are some of the titles: *On the State*, an imaginary discussion between Scipio Aemilianus and his friends, and surviving only in mutilated form; *On the Laws*, a discussion between Cicero, Atticus, and Quintus Cicero; *On the Ends of Good and Evil*, another discussion in which Epicurean, Stoic, and Academic views are stated and criticized; *The Tusculan Disputations*; *On the Nature of the Gods*; *On Old Age* (Scipio and Laelius visit Cato and listen to his wisdom); *On Friendship*; *On Duties*. These are some of the titles of what are commonly called his philosophical works – many of them are essays and musings and rambles enlivened by anecdote rather than set and methodical treatises. Throughout these writings Stoicism finds explicit and incidental treatment; thus in the *Academica* a general view of Zeno's teaching is given, in *On the Nature of the Gods* (Book ii) Stoic physics is treated, in *On the Ends* (Book iii) Stoic ethics.

Before speaking of the teachings of Stoicism, we may glance briefly at three of its later exponents. Of Seneca's public career, of his life at the court of Nero, of his wealth, and his death as an alleged conspirator against the life of Nero, we must say nothing; nor can we review the estimates of him made by modern critics, some of whom loathe him as the supreme embodiment of a nauseating hypocrisy, while others regard him as a saint – 'this pagan monk, this idealist, who would have been at home with St Jerome or Thomas à Kempis', who felt an 'evangelistic passion, almost approaching St Paul's, to open to these sick perishing souls the vision of a higher life through the practical discipline of philosophy'. The best thing to do is to take his works as they stand and judge them on their merits. There are several treatises with such titles as *On Providence*, dealing with the age-long question why the good suffer; they do not suffer, says Seneca, in the ways that really matter; *On Anger*; *On the Life of Happiness*; *On Tranquillity of Mind*; *On Mercy*, addressed to Nero and the source of some of Shakespeare's ideas in Portia's great speech; *On Kindness*. Besides this he wrote (*a*) the *Natural Questions*, which, if of no value scientifically, has some excellent descriptions of natural phenomena, (*b*) tragedies, of great influence in European tragedy, and (*c*) letters to Lucilius. The letters, which are a hundred and twenty-four in number, are musings or meditations or essays upon 'serious subjects' rather than letters; sometimes they start with an anecdote or some real happening to Seneca or Lucilius, and it is not long before the sermon follows.

Here are some samples:

All you write to me and all I hear leads me to have high hopes of you; you don't rush about or disturb yourself by moving from one place to another. All that knocking about is the sign of a sick mind; the first proof of a composed mind is that it can stay still and linger with itself. Be sure, too, that reading many authors and reading books of every type does not argue some quality of restlessness and instability. There are certain works of genius on which you ought to linger and nourish yourself if you want to take away from them something which will settle down faithfully in your mind. The man who is everywhere is nowhere. Those who spend their lives travelling about end by having many acquaintances to stay with but no real friends. The same is bound to happen if you do not attach yourself with real intimate knowledge to some one man of genius, but hurriedly scamper over everything at breakneck speed. Nothing does such harm to health as perpetual change of remedy; no wound comes to a scar if new kinds of dressings are frequently tried, and a plant never grows strong which is often transplanted. Nothing is so beneficial that it can profit you as it passes by. A multitude of books distracts the mind; since you cannot read the books you have, it is enough to have what you can read ...

And so on.

... There is no need to lift your hands to Heaven, no need to get round a temple-keeper to admit you close to the ears of the statue in the belief that you can make sure your petitions are heard: God is close beside you, he is with you, he is within you. I assure you, Lucilius, the sacred breath [*which animates the Universe*] resides within us, watching and guarding the good and evil in us; as we treat it, so it treats us. No one is a good man apart from God. Can anyone rise above fortune without God's aid? It is he who grants us counsel which makes us great, and counsel which is upright. In every good man God dwells, though we know not what god. Suppose you come across a thick wood of old trees, unusually lofty, shutting out the sky with their dense interlacing branches; the height of the wood, the hidden loneliness, the awe-inspiring shadows, heavy and unbroken when all around is open, make you believe in a divine being. A cave eaten deep into the rocky side of the mountain frowning over it, a cave not made with hands but hollowed out by nature's causes into its roomy measurements, will send a stab of religious awe through your heart. ... Suppose now you see a man unaffrighted by danger, untouched by desires, happy in adversity, calm in the midst of storm, looking upon men from a higher level, and upon gods from an equality, will not a feeling of veneration for him fill your mind? Will you not say 'This is too great and exalted a thing for me to suppose it of the same order as this little bodily frame in which it is'? A divine power has descended into it; this pre-eminent mind, so controlled, passing lightly over all things in the knowledge that they are of less worth, laughing at our fears and our hopes, surely it is possessed by power from heaven; so great a thing cannot stand so firm without support that is divine. It lives – with that part of it which is greatest – in the heaven from which it descended.

Very different from Seneca is Epictetus – a slave of Nero, later freed and eventually driven from Rome with other philosophers. He settled at Nicopolis in Epirus where in poverty and physical infirmity he lectured. He is said to have been a close friend of Hadrian, the Emperor; notes from his lectures have been preserved to us by Arrian. His was a deeply religious mind unsupported by any conviction of personal immortality. He was content to do the will of God in this world and to look no further. The burning intensity of his beliefs is expressed in violent and passionate language: ironical, pungent, epigram-matic, he shoots out questions which search into the hearts of his audience, or else he issues his indignant decrees. He must have been a lively lecturer.

From the ex-slave in his lecture room indignantly ar-raigning his motley audience we move to the tent of the Emperor Marcus Aurelius at Carnuntum, in Pannonia, where all unwillingly he shouldered his duty to turn him-self from a meditative student into the commander of an army defending the Northern frontier of the Roman Em-pire. And conscientiously and successfully he did it. But at times he withdrew into himself; and, as he fought with some of his problems in the melancholy places of his mind, he jotted down his musings and wrestlings and resolutions, and by some queer accident his jottings have come down to us. Some critics account *To Himself* – for such is the title of his meditations – as one of the world's great books;

others see in it merely the morbid haverings of a priggish mind torturing itself by its own introspective irresolution. There are twelve books which will enable the reader to decide for himself, and here are two samples :

Nothing is so productive of greatness of mind as the power to examine methodically and honestly all the things that befall us in life and to examine them, as they occur, in such way as to form an estimate of the kind of universe to which they belong, of the purpose which they fulfil in it, of their value in relation to the whole and in relation to man, who is a citizen of the highest State, of which all other states are, as it were, households : what each really is and what it is composed of and how long, judged by its own nature, it is likely to last – I mean, I should form this estimate of what now at this very moment is presented to my consciousness. And I should ask what virtue I should employ to meet it with, as for example, gentleness, courage, truth, confidence, simple naïveté, independence.

What is it you complain of? Man's wickedness? Ponder this judgement – rational creatures have been created for one another, and forbearance is part of justice; it is all unwillingly that men sin; think how many people after a life of bitter hostility, suspicion, hatred, and skirmishing with one another have been laid out in death and been burnt to ashes – think of this and then at last stop your complaints. Do you complain of the portion assigned to you out of the whole sum of things? Recall again the alternative 'Either Providence or Atoms', and all the proofs that the Universe is a kind of State.

Roman Stoicism is an attitude to life based on a few fundamental ideas variously expressed. It is not necessarily a religion, though it may take a strongly religious form : it is not a philosophical system, for the Roman exponents of it laid little stress on this aspect and express points of view which are not easily reconcilable. Nor is it a body of carefully enunciated ethical doctrine. Still less is it a mere reflection of Greek Stoicism; for, in this as in most other things, the Romans put their own imprint on what they 'borrowed'. Stoicism is the result of the contact of Eastern influences upon classical thought. The Platonic and Aristotelian schools broke up into many fragments, concerned not with the fundamental notions which had engaged their founders (for no genius arose to deal with those), but with subsidiary matters left over when the great problems were excepted. Thus, philosophy was increasingly occupied with the immediate problems of the daily behaviour of the ordinary man and not with the deeper questions upon which, in the mind of the thinker, the bases of all behaviour should logically rest. Now the tendency of the East had been to base morality, not upon a philosophical justification, but upon the authority of the prophet or seer whose intuition or moral sensitiveness seemed to carry its own credential. Thus Stoicism, and particularly Roman Stoicism, paid little attention to a basic philosophy and built up a large body of precept. Though reference was made to one or two fundamental postulates, what really carried authority was the example or the teaching of the Stoic 'wise man' or sage (*sapiens*), the man who possessed the Stoic insight into the canons of moral behaviour. 'What will the "sage" do in such and such circumstances?' is the Stoic criterion, whereas the earlier Greek question was 'How am I to discover by an intellectual process what is right and therefore what is right in this particular case?'

It would be unprofitable to set out the slender teachings on physics and logic and psychology with which the Stoic made play, or to expose their inconsistencies. It must be enough to say that to them the important thing for man was that 'he should live according to Nature', and Nature was that Force or Providence or Reason or Fate which ordains that things shall be as they are. Sometimes it was spoken of as God, sometimes God was equated with

Nature and Stoicism became Pantheism. Man's hope of happiness lies in subordination to this all-pervading and life-sustaining Power. (The reader who remembers what was said about 'subordination' in the first chapter will see why Stoicism particularly appealed to the Romans; and, if he also remembers their tendency to canonize their national heroes, and particularly Cato, he will not be surprised at the authority of the 'sage'.) The gods of popular mythology are held to be the popular version of this Universal Reason, and Reason in this context means vital principle rather than anything purely intellectual. The oneness of this principle has its implications – the unity of mankind and the brotherhood of man, and the potential equality of men, and from these ideas inferences may be drawn about nationality and politics. On the problems which may occur to the ordinary man, such as God, immortality, free-will, and death, Stoicism vacillated; sometimes God is Fate, sometimes a personal and loving deity; sometimes man is a spark of the Divine, sometimes a speck of dust; sometimes the soul is immortal, sometimes it is consumed at the final conflagration; sometimes life must be drunk to its bitter dregs, sometimes suicide is extolled. Yet upon these insecure doubts a noble ethical ideal is built. Neither trouble nor tribulation distresses the sage. He is superior to riches and poverty, to opinion critical and friendly; he does all for conscience' sake. He is kind to friends and to enemies merciful, and his forgiveness outstrips requests for it. His neighbours, whether in city or state or the world, he respects, and he does nothing to reduce their liberty. He will depart this world with the consciousness that in independence of spirit he has borne alike its joys and its sorrows and that death holds no terrors. Such was precept: in fact, the result was that, at the best, the sage tended to isolate himself from the world despite many protestations that he should take part in its activities; at the worst, he planted himself on a pinnacle of smug self-complacency and contempt of his fellows. In the first century, owing to causes into which we cannot go, Stoicism generally implied opposition to the Emperor : in the second century Emperors were themselves Stoic in sympathy and outlook.

As an answer to the urgent moral and religious hunger of the times Stoicism failed. It offered no grounds of belief and attempted to tread a hazardous tight-rope of suspended judgement. It offered a noble ideal, but no reason for enthusiasm, no motive of affection or sympathy. It demanded that a man should save himself by his own resources, in calm detachment, ignoring the desperate cries of a world protesting that salvation was not contained within it. To the sage all was easy; but how to become a sage? and no clue was forthcoming. A few might achieve an ethical integrity based upon no sanctions and find satisfaction in their sad and melancholy resignation; there was nothing for people of vigorously pulsing life, with a measureless capacity for good and evil, and with energy and strong hate and love, anxiously seeking help wherever they thought they could find it – in astrology and magic, in the ritual and lustrations and promises of alien cults, in popular nostrums and secret superstitions. And so the multitude despised the Stoic philosopher for his barren gospel.

But historically Stoicism has been a powerful influence, and it must not be underrated. Three points may be made.

First, the extraordinary closeness of very many precepts of Seneca to passages in the New Testament is evidence of the high level of morality of which the Stoic doctrine was capable. Many authors have set out in parallel columns passages from each source bearing close kinship in form and sentiment. 'Cast from you whatsoever things rend your heart: and if you could not extract them otherwise, you should have plucked out your very heart with them.' 'Love cannot be mingled with fear.' 'That gift is far more welcome which is given with a ready hand than that which is given with a full hand.' 'Let us so give as we should wish to receive.' Tertullian calls Seneca 'often our own', St Jerome 'our own Seneca', and in the fifth century letters between St Paul and Seneca were forged to account for the resemblances of thought and expression. Modern criticism accounts for them in other ways. But the influence of the writings of Seneca and Marcus Aurelius has been very great; Montaigne, for example, owes a great deal to them. For they seemed to offer a noble ethic free from the unacceptable dogmas of religion; forms of Stoicism under other names survive today.

Secondly, the influence of Stoicism on law was profound. Many of the best educated and most thoughtful Romans were Stoics, and many were also lawyers. The 'civil law' of Rome, i.e. the law operating among citizens, had gradually been broadened as the Romans came in contact with other nations possessing their own systems of law and custom; resemblances attracted attention and suggested that there might be some common basis of common notions upon which a wider law might operate, to the advantage of an Empire which was always drawing closer. Hence came the idea of a 'law of nations'. But the Stoics had yet a wider idea; their ideal was 'to live according to Nature', and Nature had a code of laws of which the philosopher could catch a glimpse. 'Natural law', it was thought, might eventually be recovered, but in the meantime the 'law of nations' was a shadowy copy of it. And so the lawyers and Stoic Emperors, in their interpretation of law rather than in new enactments, brought the law into closer touch with what they conceived to be 'natural law';

and thus the idea of 'natural law' was started upon its long history in European thought.

Thirdly, the Stoic notion of the brotherhood of man had great influence upon the treatment of slaves. We have already seen that slavery was mitigated under the early Empire, and indeed might carry, in special circumstances, positive advantages; to this change the influence of Stoicism contributed much. The xlviith letter of Seneca deals with the attitude which a Stoic master should adopt towards his slaves.

In the Greco-Roman civilization of the Empire there were many other philosophies which a man might adopt – the Cynic, the neo-Platonist, besides adaptations of Platonism and Scepticism and amalgamations of many others. Their study is of great value; Plotinus, the greatest of the neo-Platonists, is of absorbing interest both in himself and in his influence. But they are outside our scope; for we are considering the Romans, and the specifically Roman philosophy was Stoicism.

CHAPTER VIII

THE AGE OF CRISIS AND RESCUE: DIOCLETIAN AND CONSTANTINE

To this most blessed age of our Lords C. Aurelius Valerius Diocletianus Pius Felix, Unconquered, Augustus, and Marcus Aurelius Valerius Maximianus Pius Felix, Unconquered, Augustus and M. Flavius Valerius Constantius and C. Galerius Valerius Maximianus, most noble Caesars and consuls, by whose virtue and foreseeing care all is being reshaped for the better . . .

FROM AN INSCRIPTION ON A COLONNADE
DEDICATED IN NORTH AFRICA

To our Lord, the restorer of the human race, extender of the Empire and of Roman dominion, founder of everlasting security, Flavius Valerius Constantinus, Fortunate, Mighty, Pious, ever Augustus, son of the deified Constantius, always and everywhere venerable . . .

FROM AN INSCRIPTION FOUND IN ROME

IN general, the first two centuries of the Empire were centuries of peaceful development; in them was done the work of romanizing the West. Some historians have pointed out that the Antonine Age was in a sense too peaceful; they have seen it as an Age of static self-complacency, in which the original impetus lost momentum till stagnation set in. No Age is really static; if men do not proclaim what it is they are trying to do in such clear tones that the historian can hear, it does not follow that they are not aiming at something, though they may be aiming at different things and may not succeed in realizing any of them till later. Looking back from the vantage point of a later Age, the historian may be able to see what ideas, due to positive or negative causes, were influencing men. By their fruits he may infer the seeds which were germinating, though the men of the day were scarcely aware of them, or underestimated their vitality.

The fourth century will present a picture very strange to one familiar only with the first and second centuries; for the Empire had passed through the anarchy and the confused ambitions of the third century and was transformed; indeed, only by the most desperate efforts of Diocletian and Constantine was it held together at all. In the light of the changes it is possible to see something of the weaknesses of the golden Antonine Age.

If so complex a period as the third century, so deficient too in good historical witness, admits of any simple clues, perhaps they may be found, first, in the movement of power and wealth and vigour away from Rome and Italy to the provinces, secondly, in the ever-growing pressure upon the frontier provinces exerted by 'barbarian' tribes. To some extent, but not wholly, these aspects of the question are related. Clearly, threat to the frontiers thrusts into prominence the importance of the frontier provinces. But apart from this the provinces had grown in wealth and power and significance. During the early centuries Rome and Italy had been the centre from which radiated Roman civilization; as that civilization was appropriated by the provinces, they became more self-reliant from many points of view – economic, military, intellectual, and even political. The new importance of the provinces at the expense of Rome and Italy was the measure of Rome's success; but her success was fraught with disaster for herself.

The factors which contributed to the turmoil and confusion of the third century were complex, and no attempt to show them at work can be made here; nor indeed is it easy to give one priority or precedence over another; they acted and reacted upon one another. In general terms they were as follows.

In the early days of the Republic the army had been recruited from Rome; then Italy was drawn upon, then the
western provinces, Spain and Gaul. As the frontiers re-
ceded, local levies supplied more and better soldiers, the
auxiliaries became more important. By the third century
A.D. the army was drawn from the very tribes which it had
once been the business of the army to hold in check –
Germans, Moors, tribes from the Danube and from Illyria
and Dalmatia. These men were scarcely romanized;
their local sympathies were strong. Stationed often for long
periods in one province they looked at the Empire from
the standpoint of their own country or province, if indeed
they did not tend to identify the Empire with their own
neighbourhood. They had less to give to the people in
whose country they might be stationed; they tended to be
an alien element aloof from the inhabitants; sometimes
they were mere soldiers of fortune entering Rome's service.
As the barbarian threat to their particular province increased, they became aware of their power, if their
resistance to that threat was successful. A victorious army
in one province might easily become jealous of its counterpart in another; rivalries grew, generals were turned into
pretenders for the Empire; the soldiers made and unmade
Emperors; civil wars, fought for no principle or ideal,
raged for long years and squandered the strength of the
whole Empire. The Emperor who emerged successful
rested his power and his safety upon a military despotism,
pampering the armies, raising their pay and gratuities,
rewarding them with lands, and suffering their petty
tyranny over the civil population. 'Appease the soldiers or
perish' was the imperial motto. And, as the army increasingly became more barbarized, so were the generals and
pretenders whom they nominated; Africans, Thracians,
Dalmatians, a Syrian, an Arab, all wore the imperial

purple of Rome; many were untutored, many scarcely set foot in Rome, few understood what they had inherited. Roman-ness (*Romanitas*) was sadly diluted.

For at all costs the army must be increased, till by the end of the fourth century it was double the size of the army of Augustus. New systems of defence, which relied no longer on the fighting line of the frontier, but upon successive points of consolidation arranged in depth, new arms, new specialist corps were demanded. For the pressure from beyond the Empire was constant and severe, and it operated at many points at once. The garrison of the province was no longer adequate; its value presupposed spasmodic and isolated attack, whereas, as pressure was intensified, a mobile striking force was required to be sent at speed to the point most threatened. The earlier policy of buying off barbarian hordes by regular subsidies, at first successful, failed as the Empire grew obviously weaker; the settling of marauding tribes inside the frontier, tried by Marcus Aurelius, for example, only made the defences less assured. And so one race was succeeded by others in growing numbers; the Carpi raided Dacia and were followed by Goths, till Dacia was surrendered and a Roman province became their home. The Goths over a long series of years drove into East Germany, Transylvania, Illyricum, and raided by sea the whole of Asia Minor, and penetrated as far into Greece as Athens and Sparta. The Juthungi reached North Italy; the Alemanni, who first appear about A.D. 210, thrust into Gaul and Italy, and for a moment appeared before Rome. Meantime, the Persian power had revived and was often victorious over the Roman armies sent to resist its depredations. The Imperial Government was struggling for survival and it could not meet the manifold threats. It is not to be wondered, therefore, that separate parts of the Empire took independent steps to save themselves, setting up states and armies of their own and defying the central government. Such were the so-called Gallic Empire, and the state of Palmyra under Queen Zenobia, who even conquered Egypt and for a short time held the chief granary of Rome in her power. Meantime, the invading hordes plundered and burnt and slew; they carried off a vast treasure of gold and precious objects, and the Empire sank into poverty. And, as happens, they often assimilated the civilization of their victims, and during these troubled years Germans and Romans drew nearer to one another in habits and culture and outlook, and the beginnings of the German-Roman states took shape.

The centre of gravity was moving east. Where the Emperor was, there was Rome, and he was most often east of the Adriatic sea. The Balkan Peninsula was the last to be romanized, and was most vitally conscious of its Romanness, whatever its interpretation might be. It furnished the most vigorous troops, and the troops created their generals, and from its generals came Emperors. The East with its inherited wealth and longer tradition of civilization inevitably exercised its influence; imperial autocracy drew upon the age-long experience of Eastern monarchy; and in face of the menace of invasion Rome was no longer strategically suitable as a headquarters of a government, now military above all else. Italy was fast becoming a province rather than a land privileged as the cradle of Rome.

The economic effects of civil war, anarchy, disintegration, devastation of land and city by invading hordes were incalculable. Already in the Antonine Age there were ominous symptoms. The once flourishing cities of the provinces found it harder to meet their expenses; imperial taxes increased; the local councillors found office increasingly a burden, for larger calls were made on their pockets.

The value of money declined; industry satisfied local needs and found no incentive to distribute more widely; production failed to see the kind of goods that were needed, and remained stagnant. With war and invasion capital was destroyed, taxes were ground out of town and countryside to pay for the war; when money was not forthcoming, goods were seized, particularly those which would supply the needs of the armies. Lands went out of cultivation for lack of labour; the hardest and least pleasant forms of work were avoided; yet the army must have supplies. Ships were impressed to carry those supplies; the civilian population was a secondary matter; the standard of living declined as imports were confined to military necessities and inflation brought its attendant evils. Yet still, though the Empire starved, the armies must be fed and armed and clothed and transported.

It is difficult in a few words to paint the picture in dark enough colours. The Empire was within an ace of falling apart and settling down in utter collapse in poverty and famine and ruin. 'Shall I marry? Am I to be sold up? Shall I have to be a member of the local Council? Shall I get my salary? Shall I quit?' These are questions put by bewildered folk to an oracle in Egypt, and preserved to us on papyri. Trivial, but eloquent of the ordinary man's state of mind. A petition to the Emperor sent from Asia Minor reads:

We are most atrociously oppressed and squeezed by those whose duty it is to protect the people ... Officers, soldiers, city magistrates and imperial agents come to our village and take us away from our work and requisition our oxen; they exact what is not due and we suffer outrageous injustice and extortion.

Yet the Empire as a single whole was saved as by a miracle. It was saved by the exertions of two men; but it was saved at the most appalling price, so appalling that historians have sometimes asked whether it had not better perished. These two men were Diocletian and Constantine. Diocletian, Emperor A.D. 284–305, of Illyrian birth, was the son of a freedman; he served in the army and was elevated to the throne by the officers. Constantine, Emperor A.D. 306–337, was also an Illyrian, the natural son of Constantius and Helena; he too was nominated Emperor by the soldiers, and had to fight for the throne. Both men were able organizers.

The measures of Diocletian, completed by Constantine, contained little that was really new, and no attempt will be made here to show the process of development. They regularized and systematized the precedents and practices of the years of stress, when the Empire was in a state of siege; they converted emergency measures dictated by the urgent needs of the crisis into the permanent structure of government. Nothing is easier for a state to do on the plea of increased protection, or security, or prevention of inflation – in short, on the plea of the continuance of the emergency. And so the state became paramount; it was interested not in the individual as an individual, but merely as a member of a trade or class or an 'interest' organized to satisfy its own economic or administrative needs. Thus each single man became, in effect, the slave of the state. The Imperial Government clamped down upon the whole Empire the bars which were to hold it together and which achieved its imprisonment.

The reforms of Diocletian and Constantine were a stupendous effort to organize, or to plan, security. And first, the security of the Emperor, that is, of the unity of the Empire.

For sixty or seventy years the imperial authority had virtually been in the gift of the soldiers, and anarchy had resulted. Now it was to be dissociated from dependence upon any sectional interest. The Emperor's person was to be remote and detached; he was rarely seen in public, he was surrounded by a court of the Oriental pattern. Court officials, with new titles, guarded his person, and admitted to audience; semi-religious ceremonial invested him with divine authority, which he wielded as the partner of God upon the throne. Augustus had claimed to be the chief citizen; Diocletian was a monarch.

How, then, to break away from dependence upon the army, and not perish at its hands? The changes in the army which had come about gradually during the last hundred years were accepted and extended and systematized. The army was no longer officered by the senatorial and equestrian orders; 'barbarians' rose to the highest posts; the career of the soldier became exclusively military and professional. The army commander no longer carried out administrative work; civil and military posts were separated; the proconsul, familiar in early days as governor of a province and also commander-in-chief, was a thing of the past. The general was dependent for his supplies on the civil administration which was responsible to the Emperor, and he was thus held in check. Henceforth the soldier was to have no touch with administration, justice, supplies, or taxation. He was a soldier pure and simple, with no inducements to meddle with other matters, which were all in the hands of imperial officials, and no opportunities to gather into his hands the resources necessary for political initiative. Strategy, tactics, weapons all changed; the auxiliaries became more honoured than the legions; cavalry, the arm of the barbarian, took precedence over infantry, for barbarians had to be fought by barbarians and by their own weapons. The frontier garrisons (*limitanei*), once the defenders and disseminators of Roman civilization and honoured as such, were now the least efficient troops, for they were recruited by forced levy from landowners, and were reinforced by hired barbarians. The troops stationed near the cities on the interior lines of communication (*comitatenses*) to form a mobile force now stood highest in repute, though the civilians of the neighbourhood were often hard tried by their exactions and rapacity.

To maintain the army the Empire was turned into a vast administrative machine designed to produce taxes. The machinery took more men out of production, and civil servants have a way of attracting to themselves more civil servants. Diocletian saw that the Empire was too large for one man to govern; there were precedents for 'associate-emperors', and so he divided the Empire and placed over half of it his partner, entitled like himself an Augustus. To each Augustus was assigned a 'Caesar', a kind of adjutant though with special territorial responsibility. The theory was that the Caesar would succeed the Augustus, and so the problem of succession would be solved. The provinces, Italy included, were now broken up into more than a hundred areas grouped into dioceses, the dioceses themselves being grouped into prefectures. Titles were changed; it is now that *comes* makes its appearance to denote official position, as e.g. the 'Count' of Africa; the dioceses were under Vicars, as e.g. 'the Vicar of Spain'; the Emperor's advisory council was the Consistorium.

One of Diocletian's most urgent tasks was the reform of the currency in order to check inflation. Closely connected with this was his attempt to fix maximum prices for goods and services. The edict, of which part survives, defines the prices for such things as food, timber, leather, textiles, cosmetics, and the like. It fixes the rates for workers, such as shipwrights, silk and wool workers, painters, primary and secondary schoolmasters, and determines a schedule of freight rates; goods on government account were to be carried at cheaper rates, which can hardly have shown a profit to the shipowner. The mints were manipulated in a way which was equivalent to the turning out of paper money by modern governments. The attempt at stabilization failed, probably because the mines were not turning out enough gold and silver to provide an effective currency of gold and silver coins.

The chief tax was paid annually in kind. The amount required was announced each year, and divided among the four prefectures; the land was surveyed in terms of productive capacity and the quota of tax was apportioned out. This preliminary survey and the collection of tax were placed as a responsibility upon the town councils, landowners, and other agents. The post of town councillor, once a coveted honour, was now a burden; for the town councillors not only did the work, but were themselves treated as guarantors of the specified tax of an area. Every five years there were special taxes, including a tax on trading profits; and indirect taxes, e.g. customs, operated perpetually. Thus, councils, landowners, business firms, and companies were forced to work as unpaid civil servants collecting the data and the taxes, very much as business houses today keep clerks and accountants as unpaid civil servants to make the returns required by the state.

But it was useless to tax if excessive taxes drove men from the work which produced the taxes. Yet, for the purposes of the state, work must be done – 'essential work'. And so labour and skill were not merely 'directed', but were tied down to the field or bench or dockyard or office. The farm labourer could not leave the farm, nor the tenant-farmer the estate; moreover, his children must be brought up to succeed him. If, overburdened by taxes, the landowner abandoned his land, the state took it, and eventually the greater portion of the Empire passed into state-ownership. In the same way factories were nationalized. Transport was an essential service; and so the voluntary associations of dockyard labourers, merchant marine, and the like were used by the state as instruments of coercion; membership must be maintained and contracts for public services must be carried out. Hence arose a caste system; no matter what his work – town councillor, soldier, factory worker, official – each was tied to his job and status, and his children after him. If by chance he did 'improve' himself and obtained a permit to change his work, he would be liable to higher taxation; he might then be ruined. Better to remain as he was. Thus, there was no incentive to enterprise or initiative or saving; the state effectively killed them all. Production fell, and with it the standard of living; the rigid uniformity of a lifeless and static mediocrity prevailed. The price of security was the absorption of the individual by the state.

The movement of the centre of gravity eastwards likewise received recognition. Diocletian had virtually made his court and headquarters at Nicomedia on the eastern coast of the sea of Marmora; for in the past the dangers had come from beyond the Danube and from Persia; Nicomedia was a strategic point. But the ancient city of Byzantium, a Dorian colony founded about 600 B.C., lay across the water, protected or approached by gates of sea and served by an incomparable harbour. Here was an impregnable site for the new Christian city of Constantine, the new capital of the new Christian Empire, Constantinople. Years were given to its building; it was adorned with works of beauty gathered from many cities, pagan works and Christian alike. But no pagan sacrifice was offered within its walls, for it was dedicated to the new faith. For nearly a thousand years it stood inviolate, till in 1204 it was taken by Crusaders professing the faith of its founder; but till then it sheltered the religion, the learning, and the power of the East Roman Empire, the so-called Byzantine civilization.

And so the Empire was held together. Diocletian and Constantine undertook a work of reconstruction, much as Augustus had undertaken it years earlier. But, whereas Augustus reconstructed by mobilizing forces and energies and goodwill to undertake a voluntary effort, the re-formers of the third century had to impose a machinery designed to extract the resources necessary for the work of government and the ensuring of security. Of contemporary literature there is little, for the spontaneity necessary to literature was lacking. In time life and letters revived; a new imagination manifested itself, but in the members rather than in the body itself, in Africa and Gaul and Egypt. It throbbed more strongly in the arteries of Christian thought and life than in the tired channels of paganism; and eventually those members detached themselves to live their own life.

CHAPTER IX

CHRISTIANITY AND THE ROMAN EMPIRE

IT was said earlier that the Romans were extraordinarily tolerant to alien religions. Why, then, did they 'persecute' Christianity, and how did the Empire eventually become Christian?

To answer this question it is necessary to go back to Judaism. Rome tried patiently to solve the problem of the Jews; she granted them every concession. Religious affairs and civil jurisdiction were in the hands of the Jewish Council, with the High Priest as president. The Jews coined their own money, but no image of the Emperor was impressed upon it; they were exempt from military service, and the few Roman soldiers stationed in Jerusalem left their standards at Caesarea. All that Rome asked was that the Jews should furnish tribute and should live in peace with their neighbours and with the strangers, chiefly Syrian Greeks, in their land. 'Gallio cared for none of these things', and that was the invariable and the right attitude for a Roman magistrate; for Rome left freedom in religious matters to her subjects. But tolerance was met by nationalism and fanaticism. Most Jews believed that to their nation would fall the dominion of the world, for Jehovah was lord of all. A few, taught by experience and by history, discarded this belief and held that Jehovah was lord of all men's minds, for all worship of whatever kind was ignorantly a recognition of Jehovah. But the last thing the average Jew understood was universality, thus differing from some of his prophets; hence ceremonies were re-

tained which made for exclusiveness and particularism.
The Jews drew close to one another, emphasizing race and
claiming exclusive possession of their own land. In
Jehovah's good time, if they were true to their faith, they
would be triumphant: for they still held to their belief
that as Jehovah's agents they would rule the world. If as
a compact nation cleaving to their religion they developed
an independence of their own, doubtless they would thus
become the more serviceable instrument in Jehovah's
hands. But patience was not in the Jew's nature, in spite of
his history; and nationalism enflamed by fanaticism was
always liable to break out. Perhaps the small size of the
Roman force in Palestine – about 3,000 men – was a
temptation not to be resisted. But into the history of these
outbreaks and into the measures taken by the Roman
Government we cannot enter.

With the Jews scattered over the Empire, chiefly no
doubt in Rome and in the centres of trade, things were
otherwise. Rival factions sometimes created disturbances,
but on the whole these Jews lived peacefully, though
neighbours might ridicule their customs. Life out of
Palestine had broadened their minds; and, though they
might make the yearly journey to the Temple at Jerusalem, they were less exclusive, less nationalist than those
who lived under its shadow. Thus, the immunity granted
by the government and the contempt of the populace combined to secure freedom for the Jewish religion.

For thirty years or so this freedom was enjoyed by
Christianity, not because freedom was consciously granted,
but because Christianity was not distinguished from Judaism either by the government or by the people. At first
the disciples continued to observe Jewish law in Jerusalem; soon the Church, as *Acts* tells us, rapidly grew from
500 to 3,000, then to 5,000; for many Jews visiting Jeru-

salem for the Feast were converted. The Christian leaders were soon driven by Jewish persecution from Jerusalem to the synagogues of Samaria and Syria; persecutors followed, Saul being among them. Soon two victories were won; henceforth the Gospel was to be preached to Gentiles and converts were freed from Jewish customs. The Apostle of the Gentiles could now carry a Gospel emancipated from Judaism, though the enmity of 'Judaizers' dogged all his travels.

St Paul travelled by the high roads of commerce and communication now made secure by the Roman peace; he visited first the Jewish communities and then preached to the Gentiles, using the Greek language of the day. His converts were mainly of the lowest social grade; and, when his preaching caused disorder, it was the Jews who excited it. He was protected by Roman officials as a Jewish sectary. Festus would have dismissed his case as 'concerning your own religion' if St Paul, when accused of treason, had not appealed to Caesar; for, as Festus saw, the issue was not one of treason but of religious observance.

But, if the Roman Government knew no distinction at this time between Christianity and Judaism, the people soon did; for it learnt that there was in their midst something more contemptible, and something more dangerous, than Judaism. By A.D. 64, the date of the persecution under Nero, the government had at last taken notice of it; for, as presented by its attackers, Christianity deservedly provoked official attention; it failed to satisfy the terms on which Rome granted tolerance.

In the first place, Christianity was particularly vulnerable to misinterpretation: secondly, Christians often deliberately invited persecution. To the Roman of the time Christians appeared to hate the human race. They looked forward to the early return of Christ when all but themselves would be destroyed by fire as being evil; and in this disaster to 'Eternal Rome' and to the hopes of mankind they seemed to glory. In the second century and onwards this attitude of mind expressed itself in a different way; Christians went out of their way to provoke enmity that they might win a crown of martyrdom. Christians came from the lower orders of society, and their teachings seemed to aim at social revolution. They masked behind secret meetings the most frightful practices – gross immorality and cannibalism (for such interpretation could be put upon the content of such passages as St John vi. 52–9). They disrupted family life, for a convert from a family would not take part in the family worship or in some elements of family life, such as amusements. They gave evidence of their belief that the world was soon to perish by their refusal to cooperate in religious festivals, to shoulder civic responsibilities, or to serve in the army. But the pagan valued his world and his civilization. Such was the popular attitude to Christianity in the second century.

The Roman Government had easy tests. Had the cult been 'recognized' under the 'Law of Associations' which forbade regular gatherings of people except under licence? If not, it was an 'unlicensed religion' and must be suppressed, for it might hide anti-social or criminal plots of the worst kind. The magistrate in the course of his duties could deal with that. But the matter became more important if treasonable activities were suspected; would the Christian make a demonstration of loyalty to 'Rome and Augustus'?

The Christian refused; the state persisted; each misunderstood the other; each started from an opposite point. To the Roman the unity of the Empire was of vital importance, and homage to 'Rome and Augustus' embodied and expressed that ideal. It was an act of political faith.

Other cults were perfectly prepared to render that homage – except the Jews, with whom as a race the Government had come to terms; but such terms could not be granted to Christians who claimed converts in every race. Besides, the Jews did render annual sacrifice in the Temple on behalf of the Emperor, and that was enough. To the Christian the act of homage to the divinity – whatever that might mean – of Rome and Augustus was an act of religious faith, and inconsistent with the Christian faith. Hence arose the misunderstanding; neither side could see the other's point of view. Moreover, there were Christians who felt that every daily act which contributed to the welfare of the state contributed to the maintenance of idolatry. Thus, one side thought in political terms, the other in religious terms; and, as the religion was quite unlike any other in its refusal to 'live and let live', conflict was inevitable. The Christian claim to universalism seemed to aim at a state within the state, spreading its propaganda in secret. The Roman point of view is eminently intelligible.

Two points must be added. Even in the earliest persecution, that under Nero in A.D. 64, the 'Name' of Christian, as representing complicity in subversive and unspeakably loathsome practices, was the cause of persecution; and the test of 'Rome and Augustus' was applied henceforth. Secondly, there seems (more cannot be said) to have been no *general* edict against Christianity in the first two centuries. Persecution was spasmodic, and extremely local; it originated chiefly as the result of breaches of the peace which brought the question to the notice of the provincial magistrate. At any rate, in A.D. 112, Pliny, governor of Bithynia, wrote to Trajan, the Emperor, asking advice. 'Is the Name punishable or only the crimes attached to the Name?' He had imposed the test of worship. Trajan replies that no universal rule can be applied; Christians must not be sought out; if they are proved to be Christian, they must be punished: anonymous accusations are not to be entertained. It appears that Trajan, in spite of the large number of Christians in Bithynia reported by Pliny, did not regard them as actively dangerous. In the reign of Antoninus Pius and Marcus Aurelius persecution was generally originated by mob fury rather than by official initiative.

But in the third and fourth centuries the relation between the Church and the Imperial Government underwent changes which were bound up with the changed circumstances of both. Persecution was now by general edict of the Emperor, and not by local exercise of magisterial initiative. The Church had grown in numbers, in power, and in prestige. 'We are but of yesterday,' said Tertullian (at the end of the second century) in a well-known passage, 'and we have filled every place belonging to you; cities, islands, fortresses, towns, assemblies, even the camps, your tribes, your electoral divisions, the palace, the Senate, the law-courts; the only thing we have left to you for yourselves is your temples.' Moreover, Christianity had taken shape both in external organization and in the clarification of its doctrine in relation to the problems of human life in the Empire. It was now the religion of some of the ablest and best-educated men of the day. The earlier language of apocalypse ('revelation'), fiercely uttered in the expectation of the Second Coming, had been replaced by the patient pleading of defence ('apologia') and exposition. Christianity met its opponents on whatever ground they might choose. Long periods of peace, which were not always to the advantage of the Church, were interrupted by spasmodic persecution; and again it must be stressed that persecution was not undertaken, any more than in the first two centuries, in the name of religion, but in the interest of the unity and well-being of the state. For Christianity was true to its early intolerance; it would not accept a place among its contemporary religions; the claim which it made upon its adherents was absolute. But in the third and fourth centuries the state was desperately concerned with unity.

The change in the relations of Christianity and the Government may perhaps be seen most quickly by glancing at the reasons which brought about the persecution. Septimius Severus was not originally hostile; indeed he gave the care of his son Caracalla to a Christian nurse; but he became alarmed by the rapid increase in the number of Christians and he forbade baptism of pagans. The prohibition lapsed after his death. The measures of Decius were more drastic; they were inspired by the growing signs of the organization of the Church as an exclusive section of society, by its pacifism and the resulting threat to the military efficiency of the Empire, and by the Emperor's desire for good relations with the Senate. Every citizen was ordered to appear before the magistrate and to make sacrifice to pagan gods and to receive a certificate that he had so sacrificed. Here is an extract from a certificate found in Egypt:

I have always sacrificed to the gods; and now in your presence [*i.e. of the officials*] and according to the terms of the edict, I have sacrificed ... and I ask you to add your signature ... I [*the official*] ... saw him sacrificing and have signed my name.

Thus the Christians were revealed; and, though fierce persecution followed for a brief time, the original intention was to cause wholesale renunciations of faith. And the edict was successful not only in causing 'lapses', but also in creating endless trouble for the churches on the question of the readmittance of the 'lapsed'; moreover, the number of Christians who fraudulently obtained certificates cast discredit upon the faith. In A.D. 257 Valerian attempted to bring about the Christian tolerance which had been refused for two centuries, by ordering the higher clergy to sacrifice, while permitting them to remain Christian in private; and in the east laymen and clergymen were punished for being Christians, especially harsh penalties being prescribed for senators and knights. The Church as an organization was thus attacked. But it was under Diocletian that the issue was most clearly defined. In his desperate efforts to cement together the Empire he was particularly sensitive to influences which tended towards separatism. Though at first he underestimated the strength of the Christians, by A.D. 303 he had reached the conclusion, under pressure from Galerius, his partner in rule, that there was indeed a state within the state. His measures went beyond precedent. No Christian could hold Roman citizenship; therefore he could hold no post in the imperial or municipal services, nor could he appeal from a judicial verdict. No Christian slaves could be freed. The churches and the sacred books were to be destroyed. This edict was followed by others. The clergy were to be imprisoned and were to be made by torture to sacrifice to the gods. The aim was to rob the laity of its leaders and the organization of the Church of its main supports. Finally, this last edict was made to apply to all Christians.

Thus, in the interest of the unity of the Empire, Christianity was to be broken up and dispersed. And the edicts, while they did not bring about the unity of the Empire, did cause disunion in the Church.

But during the years which followed, the unity of the Empire was threatened rather by the open conflict of rival Emperors; and in A.D. 311 the next stage was reached in the relations of Church and Empire.

Nevertheless, because great numbers still persist in their opinions, and because we have perceived that at present they neither pay reverence and due adoration to the gods, nor yet worship their own God, therefore we ... have judged fit to ... permit them again to be Christians. ... It will be the duty of the Christians ... to pray to God for our welfare and for that of the public and for their own ...

This was the 'Edict of Toleration' issued by Galerius, a former persecutor, as he lay dying of a frightful disease. But it was the so-called Edict of Milan, A.D. 313, which put the matter on a new and regular basis – the religious neutrality of the state. It is possible that no such pronouncement was issued as an edict; but, as given by the historian Lactantius, the 'Edict' certainly sums up authentically the instructions sent by the Emperor Constantine to his officials during the years A.D. 311–13. Its drift can be gathered from these extracts:

... no man should be denied leave of attaching himself to the rites of Christians or to whatever other religion his mind directed him, that thus the supreme divinity, to whose worship we freely devote ourselves, might continue to vouchsafe his favour and beneficence to us ... The open and free exercise of their respective religions is granted to all others, as well as to the Christians ... and we mean not to derogate aught from the honour due to any religion or its votaries.

All Church property was to be restored, even at a cost to the imperial exchequer. And at the same time the Emperor Constantine declared himself a Christian, and without persecuting paganism weighted the scales of neutrality strongly in favour of Christianity.

The Roman Government had been puzzled about Christianity. It took time to discover the new faith; it had discovered it and misunderstood it. Through misunderstanding it had applied an impossible test; the test refused, it persecuted spasmodically; intermittent persecution seemed to serve only as a stimulant; the first general persecution was too late; neutrality was now the only course, and it remained the permanent policy for sixty years. Emperors might be pagan, and, indeed, like Julian the Apostate (A.D. 361), might give all encouragement to paganism, just as Constantine before him had supported the Christian Church; but neutrality officially prevailed. In A.D. 378 the last step was taken by Theodosius, who surrendered neutrality and proscribed paganism. The temples were nationalized, and became museums of art. The calendar, hitherto based on pagan festivals, was reformed. The gods were legislated out of existence, though not without opposition. The state employed the same instrument in favour of Christianity which had been employed against it in the previous century. And paradoxically the state was influenced by the same motive as before. Whereas, earlier, in the supposed interest of the survival of the Empire as a unity held together by religious sanctions, it had persecuted Christianity, now, with the same purpose it strove to stamp out the enemies of Christianity. Hope of the success and survival of the Empire depended on that which had once been thought to be disruptive of imperial unity and welfare. The state placed itself under the aegis of the Christian religion, the religion of a minority of its members. Thus, the state was true to the belief of the Romans of the early Republic, that Rome depended upon the goodwill of divine power. So, it might be said, had primitive Roman faith vindicated itself.

So momentous and so sudden a reversal of policy as came about in A.D. 313 cannot be explained as the inevitable and almost predictable result proceeding from sufficient causes. The historian, tracing the course of things and assessing the nature of men's thoughts, is suddenly startled by an event for which he is totally unprepared.

The change was brought about by one man, Constantine, whose character refuses to fit into the pattern of the age, whose convictions are uniquely his own, whose very language, as shown in letters and rescripts, is new and unexpected. Twenty or so years after the persecution by Diocletian, Constantine, the Roman Emperor, writes such sentences as are quoted below (the circumstances in which they were written cannot here be narrated):

divisions of this kind [*in the Church*] should not be kept from me, for by them the high God may be moved not only against the human race, but also against me myself to whose care by His heavenly will He has entrusted the guidance of all the affairs of earth, and so may in anger decide things otherwise than hitherto. For then indeed shall I be able to be most fully free from anxiety and to hope to receive always all that is most prosperous and best from the ready generosity of the most powerful God, when I shall see that mankind, held together in brotherly unity, adores the most holy God with the worship of the Catholic religion, as is due to Him.

The result [*of schism*] is that the very men who ought to preserve brotherhood in unity of mind and spirit stand apart from one another in a shameful and wicked feud and so provide those who keep their minds turned away from this most holy religion with an excuse for mocking at it.

The Gospel books and the Apostles' books and the prophecies of the ancient prophets teach us clearly what we ought to think about the Divine. Therefore let us drive away the strife which creates war and let us find the solution of our problems in those divinely-inspired writings.

The eternal and divine goodness of our God which is past understanding by no means permits the conditions of mankind to wander too long in darkness, nor does it allow the hateful wills of some men to prevail so long that it will not open afresh to them by its own most brilliant lights a road to salvation, nor grant to them conversion to the rule of righteousness. I know this full well from many examples, and I can gauge it from my own case ... Of a

truth I cannot describe or enumerate the blessings which God of
His divine generosity has granted to me, His servant. I rejoice
therefore, in particular I rejoice, that ... you [*the Emperor's 'most
dear brothers, the Catholic bishops'*] have recalled to a better hope
and a better state those whom the malignity of the devil seemed
by his persuasion to have turned from the glorious light of the
catholic law. O truly victorious providence of Christ the Saviour.

These brief extracts have been given because there is no
more expeditious method of revealing the rapid change
which has come over the thought and language of the
fourth century as compared with those of the second century.

Here was a Roman Emperor who had identified himself with Christianity, the Christian Church, and the
Christian Creed, who was convinced of a mission from
which he could not escape, laid by the Christian God upon
him as His servant, who devoted patience and energy to
the cause for unity within the Church as an essential condition of the unity and prosperity of the Roman state, who
was not content even with a united Church but felt himself charged with a special duty towards 'those outside' to
bring them within the fold of a truly catholic Church.

At first, Christianity was preached to the lowest orders of
society living upon the high roads of communication; by
the end of Constantine's reign it had penetrated into the in-
nermost parts of the Empire, and up to the highest levels.
At first it laid stress on the immediate return of Christ, and
its language was the language of 'apocalypse'; later it took
a longer view, and reasoned defence and explanation of its
doctrines brought the Gospel to the educated; and attack
– the best means of defence – assailed the foundations of
paganism. Its attitude to works of pagan literature and
learning had at first been uncompromising, for they were
the bible of paganism. After struggles of conscience the

ablest men of the Church realized that pagan literature was separable from paganism, and that Christianity could not refuse itself the aid of education and scholarship. In the early part of this period of three hundred years the hostility of the people had set in motion the repressive measures of the state; in the latter part the state, more nervously solicitous for imperial unity than in the Principate, itself took the initiative, while Christian and pagan on the whole settled down in peace with one another under an all-pervasive domination. In so far as originality of thought and expression survived, the advantage lay with Christianity; for, while pagan thought and letters and religion could only plough again familiar acres now almost exhausted, Christianity had a new interpretation of life to offer, and its vitalizing message transformed old modes of thought and language. Even before the reign of Constantine the Church held property, though under what legal title is obscure. From persecution to neutrality to favour; from degradation to respectability to dignity; from unquestioning faith to statements of creed couched in the most searching of philosophical terms; from ignorance to learning. Henceforth the Christian Church was armed with all the panoply which Greco-Roman civilization could furnish for the next period of its history. But that is the chapter of the Middle Ages, though in a very real sense still the history of Rome.

CHAPTER X

THE FIFTH CENTURY

Neither grey hairs nor wrinkles can suddenly take away moral authority; a life honourably lived reaps its rewards of authority to the end.
                                                                    CICERO

WE now pass to the beginning of the fifth century, not in order to give an outline of events, but to look back from that standpoint upon some of the changes which had taken place in Roman institutions and ideas. For present purposes all that need be recorded between A.D. 337 (the death of Constantine) and A.D. 400 is that a brief attempt had been made by Julian to revitalize paganism, that Theodosius had established Christianity as the official religion, that in A.D. 395 his two sons had divided the Empire into two parts, Arcadius ruling in the East and Honorius in the West, and that the pressure of Huns and Goths upon the northern frontier of the Danube had become severe and alarming.

In the sphere of government and public life the old ideals have passed away, though the names remain, a shadow without substance; the reign of Diocletian and its inauguration of the all-powerful state had in fact destroyed all that Cato or Cicero, or even Pliny, had regarded as an essential characteristic of Rome.

The partnership of Augustus and the Senate had gradually broken down; the position of Princeps had become more autocratic during the first century; and, though for a moment under the Antonines the Senate had dreamed of a restoration of its position when it exercised influence in the choice of an Emperor's successor, those dreams had been shattered in the third century by the army's usurpation of authority. After Diocletian the Senate, though it might meet as a council, gradually became an 'order of society', enjoying certain exemptions from taxes and certain dignities. Very many members of this order had never seen the city of Rome or even travelled outside the provinces in which they were born. From being an 'order' of men elected by the people to magistracies and so qualified to sit in the great council of the Republic, which in fact though not by right had governed the Roman world, senators became a stratum of society, enjoying privileges but no power. They drew away from other men, aloof and self-contained, and cast back their minds to the traditions and the literature and culture of an age which they fondly thought could never really pass away. The power of the Emperor, girt about with the sanctity, first, of 'divinity' and later of vice-regency as God's representative, was absolute and was not called into question. The hope of a Republican restoration which the senators of the early Empire had cherished had now long been forgotten. Yet the old phrases are kept; when in A.D. 458 the Emperor Majorian writes, purely out of politeness, to the Senate, he addresses them as *patres conscripti*, 'enrolled fathers', the most ancient name of the Senate dating from the early days of the Republic. He acknowledges that the Senate has chosen him and the army has ordained his appointment. He describes himself as *Princeps*, the title used by Augustus; yet he also speaks of his *regnum*, his position as *rex*, the title abhorred by Romans, and he hopes to serve faithfuly the *respublica*, the ancient name for the commonwealth, which has compelled him to reign.

Roman citizenship had once been a valued possession. In the early days of the Republic citizenship had been fought for and won; in the last century of the Republic 'allies' of Rome had wrested it from an unwilling donor. The appeal made in virtue of his Roman citizenship by the greatest Roman citizen of the first century A.D., St Paul, had received immediate attention. The dignity of that status, as well as its rights and duties, had been the creation of a long process of political development, which had come to its full stature under the early Empire. It was already declining when the Emperor Caracalla enfranchised virtually the whole of the Roman world, in order that the whole world might pay the taxes due from a Roman citizen. And now the idea of citizenship had vanished; the municipal towns no longer cherished a valued civic life, they bore only the burdens of taxation; and town councillors had exchanged the pride of office for the enforced responsibility of tax-collection. Men were finding in membership of the Christian Church the sense of citizenship which neither Rome nor municipality could any longer offer them.

Many of the great offices of state, the magistracies, had disappeared or had been so altered as not to be the same offices except in name. The function of the praetor was now to organize public shows; once he had been a high judicial authority. The consulship was a high honour – for it was bestowed by the Emperor – and was nothing more; yet in A.D. 399 it was so valued that it is called a 'Divine reward'. The great provincial commands, formerly the last honour and the heaviest responsibility of those who had served the state in a series of magistracies to which they were elected by the people, became rungs in the ladder of promotion ascended by the professional civil servant employed by the Emperor. Their original powers and duties were divided and placed in the hands of separate officials, all acting as a check upon one another. Once the provinces owed their romanization in great part to the enlightened policy of able administrators; now the civil servant was hated, for his function was to extort taxes, to see that none left his appointed guild or sought other work or evaded tribute to the state in money or kind or services. The state was the universal master. In the early days of the Republic, when the plebeians had demanded a champion, they forced upon the patricians the creation of tribunes to safeguard their interests. And now the oppressed found their protection again, not in a magistrate of the state, but in the persons of the bishops of the Church. Popular demand forced upon men of its choice the role of bishop; St Ambrose, Bishop of Milan, was not even baptized when he was compelled by the crowd to shoulder the responsibilities of this office. The letters of men like St Ambrose and St Augustine show clearly the work of the bishops. They resist official tyranny, they withstand provincial governors, with whom personally they are often on friendly terms, they take matters to the imperial ear itself, they arbitrate in disputes and guide and guard their peoples in all the difficulties of their lives. It is now that the Church becomes the leader in the alleviation of poverty and distress, in providing hospitals and schools and orphanages and charity of all kinds. And so it offered to men a hope and belief that the individual still was of worth, though society might be in bondage to the state. The bishop virtually took over the functions of the city magistrate who by this time was an unwilling tool of the Government; and the bishop was the choice of the city population.

As for the army, formerly it was the Roman's privilege to fight as citizen and protector of his family and his gods on behalf of the city of Rome. The cavalry had taken precedence, then later the legionary. But the growing needs of Empire had changed this; first the professional army, then the recruitment of non-Roman elements, and finally the barbarization of the army. Now, barbarian kings were employed to defend the frontiers at a price; the least civilized of the provincials were swept into the army with all the remnants of the population that were not exempted by other forms of services essential to the state. From being an apostle of romanization the soldier, and no less his officer, was now the roughest and most uncilivized element of the Roman world. Discipline was harsh and merciless, as the enactments of the Code of Theodosius show. The most honoured arm was the cavalry, now protected in armour and mail, from which the panoplies of Arthur's Knights of the Round Table were directly derived.

Land was passing out of the hands of the smallholders, and of farmers on a moderate scale. The state confiscated what it needed or found to be unproductively managed. Landowners annexed neighbouring estates which could not produce what the revenue collectors demanded; for the state was concerned not so much with maintaining titles to ownership as with ensuring that the land paid tribute in tax or kind or in the services of the labourers upon it. Huge domains passed into the hands of one family; and thither flocked the former middle classes in order to secure, as virtual serfs, a livelihood and some protection from the attentions of the state: for often the landowners were able to evade or to defy the Government officials. Moreover, the corruption and bribery were on a colossal scale, as the Theodosian Code shows; the Emperor tried to check them by enactments from the seat of government, but his authority was impotent. The bailiffs of the large estates made their arrangements with officials, sometimes cheating their employers, sometimes in collusion with them, sheltering deserters from the army, rendering false returns with the connivance of land inspectors. The picture is terrible.

Yet it was precisely on these large estates owned by the country aristocracy that culture of the old kind flourished. In Gaul and Africa the landowners lived a secluded life in their luxurious houses, corresponding with one another (for letters were greatly in vogue as a form of literature), discussing the literary merits of the classical writers Vergil, Horace, Terence, Statius, and the rest. There were centres of academic studies throughout the Empire; and Gaul, especially, could claim several of note, in particular that at Bordeaux. Literature was the favourite study, philosophy languished. But in spite of the aridity of much of this study it was pursued with an earnestness which is in a sense pathetic; for it proceeded from two contradictory and sub-conscious feelings – first, that the old culture was passing away; secondly, that it could never pass away, for then nothing but void could be imagined.

Rutilius Claudius Namatianus was a member of one of the Gallic noble families, whose estates were 'made ugly' by the invading barbarians. His father had held office in Rome and he himself had been Prefect of the City in A.D. 413, six years after the law condemning paganism and four years after Alaric's descent upon Rome. In a poem of 700 lines he tells the story of his unwilling return from Rome to Gaul to look after his lands, with what reluctance he tore himself away from the city 'where the sky is clearer above the seven hills', and as he leaves he utters amid his tears a grateful prayer :

Rome is the Queen of the world, nurse of men and mother of gods, whose majesty shall not fade from the hearts of men till the sun itself is overwhelmed : her gifts are as widely spread as the sun's rays – the sun which rises and sets on lands ruled by Rome. Her advance was held back neither by the scorching desert nor the icy armoury of the north: wherever Nature had fostered life, there Rome had penetrated. She had made one fatherland of many nations, and to be brought within her rule was a blessing. What was before the world Rome had turned into one city, offering the conquered partnership in her own law. Clemency had tempered her might of arms: whom she had feared, she had overcome, and whom she had overcome she loved. Embracing the whole world in her law – bringing victories, she had made all things live together joined in a common confederacy. Other empires had waxed and waned: but Rome's war had been righteous, her peace free from pride, and glory had been added to her vast resources. Her deeds had exceeded her destiny: what she ruled was less than she deserved to rule ... And then Rutilius calls upon Rome to summon to her aid her old courage and fortitude ... Despite the pain, the wounds will heal and the limbs grow strong. From adversity snatch prosperity, from ruin riches. The heavenly bodies set, only to renew their light: what cannot sink leaps most quickly to the surface: the torch is dipped that it may blaze more brightly. The foes of Rome, for a moment victorious, were routed one and all and even Hannibal lived to regret his success. The disaster which wrecks others renews Rome; her power to thrive in calamity will give her a second birth. Her enemies shall be brought low, and eternally for Rome the Rhineland shall be ploughed, the Nile shall overflow its banks, and Africa and Italy and the West shall lavish corn and wine.

The poem breathes much of the atmosphere of the Rome of four centuries earlier; the gods are there, the myths: places exercise their old charm, the old institutions receive due reverence, and the 'ancient ways' still delight:

the magic of Rome pervades all. There is no hint that the old order has passed, Christianity receives no mention; there is still the faith that Rome can emerge triumphant. Rutilius is not alone, either as a devoted Roman or as a provincial devoted to Rome. Claudian, who was born in Egypt, cared not whether the Western Emperor was Christian or pagan so long as he was Emperor of Rome, for the Eastern upstart, Constantinople, he detested: his passion was the Senate and the pagan institutions for which it stood. He also obstinately clung to the past, and from the past created a Roman future. The letters of Symmachus, too, relate in placid calm the trivialities of the day, and assume the maintenance of the priestly colleges and the ordered routine of the ancient worship. Yet he lived on friendly terms with some of the most uncompromising enemies of paganism. And there were many others like him.

There was, however, another place besides the houses of Gallic nobles in which the culture of Greco-Roman civilization was preserved – within the Christian Church itself, in the bishops' houses and schools, in monasteries, in Church foundations, and even in hermits' cells. As is well known, there had been a division of opinion among Christian writers and thinkers; some, like Tertullian, were for destroying all that was pagan in origin; others, like Clement of Alexandria, were for 'spoiling the Egyptians'. By the fifth century this conflict had largely been resolved; and Christian leaders were often the best-educated men of the day. In these centres there was life and enterprise; the Roman training in rhetoric found a new outlet in the sermon and the theological treatises, which were often published in instalments eagerly awaited by their readers. Disputes with pagan supporters of the old learning gave opportunity for polemical pamphlets, while the necessary and voluminous correspondence of men like St Augustine and St Jerome gave new reality to this form of writing.

In this way it would be possible to summarize the changes which have taken place in the principal Roman ideas and institutions. But the real nature of these changes can be seen only by a reading of some of the literature of the time, as e.g. the letters of Symmachus and Sidonius and St Augustine and St Jerome. But there remains one topic which may receive slightly fuller treatment, namely the fate of Roman religion.

As the Empire expanded to include the Mediterranean area, new cults and rituals and philosophies had spread from one end to the other, some indigenous to the area, others coming from Persia and the further East. The worship of the Great Mother we have already spoken of earlier; but hosts of other deities claimed worship – Mithras the Sun-god of Persia, Isis and Osiris, gods from Egypt, the god of Syria, who was called Jupiter Dolichenus, and the like. There are the gods of the countryside, Italian and provincial, with names and cults going back into pre-Roman times, the gods of the state, Jupiter, Juno, Minerva, and the rest; vague powers, Fortune, Tutela, Genius in manifold forms; abstract ideas like Fides, Concordia; gods peculiar to districts and localities like some of the Gallic gods. And gods borrowed and combined names and rituals and legends. And all these cults – and they run into hundreds – were carried on in spite of the nominally Christian Empire. Emperors might persecute them, but they persisted and the imperial authority was powerless. For the Roman noble families insisted on the maintenance of the gods of the Republic, and popular sentiment and habit would not part with traditional superstitions. Society as a whole – except the sincere Christians, and it must not be forgotten that there were many nominal Christians – kept alive ancient Roman cults for one overwhelming reason, that the continuance of the Roman state seemed to depend upon the continuance of the Roman gods and their worship. Personal religion might be satisfied by any other worship, but the Roman rites which had been handed down for centuries must go on; for the whole structure of organized life depended on them. And organized life – in fact, touch with the 'ancient ways' – had been almost destroyed in the troublous times of the third century. At all costs it must be preserved, and it could be preserved only in the hallowed forms of religion, and in the literature and the sentiments which enshrined those forms. The noble families handing on traditional culture had watched religion after religion becoming popular; Emperors had associated themselves with the cult of the Sun-god, of Hercules, of Syrian Baal, and others; the last was Christianity, but there was no reason why it should continue. The Emperor Julian's reversion to paganism was a good sign; and, though he had failed to destroy Christianity as the 'official' religion, what he had attempted could be successfully achieved later. But in fact it was not the existence of Christianity or any other cult which the champions of pagan culture detested; for there was a large and easy tolerance, and, as one of them said, there is 'no one road to so great a secret'. What they opposed was the Christian hatred of the old Roman cults which had gone on for centuries and which had been the guarantee of the stability of Rome.

But they meant much more than this. When Ennius had said that the welfare of 'Roman things' stood rooted in the ancient ways and in the sterling quality of Rome's men, he had in mind Rome as he knew it. Since then the horizon had broadened; the whole of Mediterranean civilization which Rome had taken under its wing was now Greco-Roman civilization and for its continuance Rome was responsible. Within Greco-Roman civilization there lay the possibility of perfection and finality. Not that the world was perfect or that human institutions were final, but within the 'thought-forms', if the phrase may be used, at which that civilization had painfully arrived – in politics, in social ideals, in ethics, and in the material expression of these things – there was the hope of perfection. This – and much more – is all contained in the phrase 'Eternal Rome'. Rome's own spiritual experience, the union of that experience with the rest of Mediterranean civilization, and the resulting new creation offered the framework within which lay the fortunes of humanity. Destroy those 'thought-forms', destroy the old culture of which the old gods were a part, and humanity was doomed.

This was the challenge which Christian writers and thinkers had to take up; and in taking it up they found themselves much embarrassed, and chiefly for two reasons. In the first place, they were themselves the product – and often the finest product – of Greco-Roman civilization; and to think beyond it and outside it implied a supreme effort of thought and will. Secondly, they owed to it the very tools with which they were going to criticize, and many of them loved pagan literature with real devotion. Thus, they were engaged upon the difficult task of an intellectual and emotional reorientation.

The point is capable of illustration from many angles; but it must suffice to consider only St Augustine, the supreme example.

Before he became a Christian, St Augustine was a teacher of rhetoric in Italy; he knew Roman literature well; he had read much Greek literature and philosophy in Latin translations. He was thoroughly conversant with

the literary and philosophic discussions of his time; he had
been deeply influenced by Manicheism, and by neo-
Platonism. After his conversion he had hoped to live a
monastic life; but he found himself exalted to the care and
responsibilities of a bishopric in his native country, Africa.
In A.D. 410, Alaric, King of the Goths, invaded Italy,
captured Rome, and withdrew. Refugees fled to the
southern coasts of the Mediterranean, bringing the news
with them. The shock to the Roman world was stupendous; it seemed that civilization was to fall in ruins. The
panic grew less as it became clear that Rome still stood,
and that things were going on much as before; for the
damage to the city was not great, the barbarians had be-
haved with unexpected moderation. The shock to sentiment remained. If Rome had been true to her ancient
gods, this catastrophe would never have happened. Such
was the indignant and frightened plea of the champions of
Roman culture.

In A.D. 413, St Augustine began to write his work *On
the City of God*, and he finished it in A.D. 426, though
portions of it appeared successively between these dates.
It was a work prompted by the times, and its primary purpose was to give guidance in their interpretation. The
scope of its twenty-two books cannot be indicated here; but
three points must be made.

First, Books i–x are devoted to the refutation of the
charge that the evils of the world are to be attributed to
the ban laid upon pagan worship by the Christians, and by
the Christian Roman Empire. For this purpose Roman
history is put under scrutiny, and the conclusion is that the
Roman gods did not in fact save Rome in other crises, and
by their very character were incapable of saving her. Nor
can the Roman gods offer anything of guarantee to the
individual soul for the life to come. This last argument is

directed against those pagans who, though not blaming Christianity for recent imperial disasters, yet thought that the old cults offered positive benefit for the future. Now St Augustine, writing a tract for the times, was not likely to fight with shadows; indeed, we are told that some pagans contemplated publishing a reply. In other words, he was fighting a powerful and widespread belief that only the maintenance of ancient cults and the culture associated with them could save civilization.

In the second place, St Augustine is a profound admirer of the Roman achievement in history and of the Roman virtues, through which that achievement had been won. Of this he leaves no shadow of doubt. Not only does he say so constantly, but all his writings are soaked through and through with classical thought, with copious illustration and reference; indeed, his point of departure is often the correct orthodox stand-point of paganism. What he does criticize in Roman character is precisely the element which he could not condone – materialism and cruelty and immorality. Whereas the pagans asserted that Roman character had *made* Roman history and Roman character was bound up with ancient religion, St Augustine admired much of Roman history, admired much of Roman character, but denied the necessary association of either with ancient religion. At the time this position was less intelligible than it might seem now; and his task was not easy. It was easier to take up Tertullian's position and to condemn outright the whole structure and thought of a civilization derived from paganism. St Augustine did not choose this way. If he had chosen it, history would have taken a different course.

But the whole question was much more profound than so far appears. For the question of the gods of Rome was only one aspect of something much larger. Once again, perhaps, the point can be put shortly by referring to a passage in the same book, *On the City of God*. St Augustine has just reviewed the various kinds of 'good' which the different philosophies of the classical world had set up as the end to be pursued. They had regarded happiness as the chief end, and some had found happiness to consist in virtue, others in pleasure of different kinds, others in the satisfaction of elementary needs, and so on.

If then the question be put to us what the City of God, if asked about all these matters one after the other, would reply, and, first, what its views are about the 'ends' of good and evil, it would reply that eternal life is the highest good and eternal death the highest evil; we must live rightly to obtain the one and to avoid the other. It is written 'The righteous man lives by faith'; for we do not see our good now; hence we must seek it in faith, nor is it possible for us to live aright out of our own resources, unless He helps our faith and our prayers who gives us the very faith to believe that help is available from Him.

'Eternal life' is used in the sense in which it is used in the Fourth Gospel, 'life of a quality which is permanent' rather than 'life without end'.

This passage may perhaps indicate the contrast between the Christian and non-Christian point of view. Greco-Roman civilization had found within the 'thought-forms' of its particular culture the final answer to humanity's needs; that is what is meant by 'Aeterna Roma'. For, though at first sight it may appear that in relying upon Roman gods for prosperity Rome was appealing to something outside herself, actually her appeal was made, as it always had been made, in order to put the gods into the way of favouring what the Romans themselves intended. The criticism which the Christians make of pagan thought is that it regards man as sufficient of himself, that the world can be explained by the world; their own creed is that, unless man invokes a principle outside himself, he can find no solution of his problems. Thus, it is no longer a matter of securing the goodwill of the gods, for the successful achievement of what men will; but of doing the will of God, for its own sake, often in violation of what men, left to themselves, would will. That is the point at issue, as the Christians saw it. But that the difference was beyond compromise did not mean that learning was therefore to be cast aside. (The point perhaps might be put shortly in this way, though this is not in St Augustine. Archimedes, when elaborating the theory of levers had said that, if only he had a point of fulcrum outside the world, he would move the world. The Christian believed that Greco-Roman thought attempted to move the world from within and naturally failed; only Christianity offered the principle from outside.)

Thus St Augustine argued with the supporters of the old Roman worship. But on a lower plane he had another task to perform, which had engaged the powers of every Christian teacher for generations; he had to wrestle with the gods and vague powers (*daemons*) who possessed the minds of the less educated – the malign 'influences' of astrology, the power of 'fortune' and luck, the 'magic' of spiritualists, the terrors of half-remembered superstitions, the cults of a thousand and one little gods. These were the enslaving forces from which the masses had to be liberated. That many native gods took on a Christian guise as patron saints is well known, and the process can be watched in some detail. But of all this no more can be said.

With St Augustine we have reached the last great name of antiquity. When he died in A.D. 430, the Vandals were overrunning Africa and were already at the gates of Hippo.

But there is one last word to be said. If the same barbarians who overran great tracts of the Roman Empire in the fourth and fifth centuries A.D. had descended the peninsula of Greece in the fifth century B.C., in all probability they would have seen and appreciated little or nothing of the special characteristics of Athenian culture, and much might have been destroyed. When they descended the Italian peninsula eight or nine hundred years later, they found a civilization which they could to some extent understand and appreciate; for part of it took the form of a massive grandeur of buildings, and roads and fortifications and ordered government. On the whole their aim was to appropriate rather than to destroy. But they had to be educated, and Latin literature was beyond their reach at the moment. Now the Romans from Cicero's time had shown a genius for composing manuals and encyclopedias. The two most famous compilers were Varro and Pliny the Elder, and henceforth the influence of these writers was enormous in every medieval centre of learning. But in the sixth and seventh centuries these works were too ambitious and therefore one writer after another wrote shorter 'summaries' of departments of knowledge. These were to be the text-books for the education of the new Western nations; and such writers as Cassiodorus (fifth century) and Isidore of Seville (sixth century) and Boethius conferred incalculable benefits upon Western civilization. As the nations grew up, they grew out of the elementary text-books; and they were able to go to Latin literature itself, stored away in libraries and monasteries and ecclesiastical centres of learning. Here they found the original Latin authors, and gained an introduction to Greek thought through Latin translations of Greek literature, till at last they were able to go to Greek literature itself.

The barbarian invasions were neither catastrophic and

sudden, nor destructive and disruptive. Rome never fell, she turned into something else. Rome, superseded as the source of political power, passed into even greater supremacy as an idea; Rome, with the Latin language, had become immortal.

CHAPTER XI

ROMAN LAW

Justice is the constant and perpetual will to give each man his right.
Digest OF JUSTINIAN

THE greatest achievement of the Romans, whether we consider it on its own intrinsic merits or in its influence on the history of the world, is without doubt their law. 'There is not a problem of jurisprudence', says Lord Bryce, 'which it does not touch : there is scarcely a corner of political science on which its light has not fallen.' 'What the American law needs most today', says an American lawyer, 'is more of the invigorating eternal influence of Roman law.' And the same writer claims that, whereas the population of the Roman Empire may have been 50 millions, at present 870 million people live under systems traceable to Roman law.

It is naturally impossible to explain satisfactorily in a short chapter why Roman law is so supreme an achievement; yet not even the slightest book on the Romans should therefore dismiss the subject. None the less, the simplest account cannot help being difficult reading.

In A.D. 527 Justinian became Emperor of the East Roman Empire, of which Constantinople was the capital. For a hundred years or so Italy had been under the control of 'barbarian' kings, Teutonic in origin. In the middle of the century Justinian's generals reconquered Italy, and till the twelfth century the East Roman Empire maintained some hold upon it.

Soon after his accession Justinian gave orders that

Roman law should be codified. The codified Roman law was published in A.D. 533 and it applied to the East Roman Empire. When Italy was recovered, it became law there also and thus it became known to the West. Eventually schools and universities came into being very largely to study it. Justinian's great work is the *Corpus Iuris Civilis*, the Corpus of Civil Law, comprising the *Code* (imperial statutes), the *Digest* (jurisprudence), the *Institutes* (an elementary treatise), the *Novellae* (later enactments from A.D. 535 to 565).

The question is: What were the qualities in Roman law which earned for it so great and permanent an influence? The answer to this question will throw light on the qualities of the men who elaborated this law.

The *Digest* opens with these words of Ulpian :

Anyone intending to study law [*ius*], should first know whence the word *ius* is derived. It was named *ius* from justice: for, as Celsus aptly defined it, law is the art of the good and the fair. It is by virtue of this that a man might call us priests; for we worship justice, and we profess a knowledge of what is good and fair, separating the fair from the unfair, discriminating between what is allowed and what is not allowed, desiring to make men good not merely by fear of penalties but by the encouragement of rewards; we lay claim, unless I am mistaken, to a true philosophy, not a sham philosophy.

These seem at first strange words, yet they were written by one of the greatest minds of jurisprudence.

Law did in fact start with the priests, in Rome as elsewhere; and Justinian, after a thousand years of Roman law, claims that lawyers might well be regarded as priests of justice. By 450 B.C. law was out of the hands of the priests : customary unwritten law was now written down in the Twelve Tables. They were published in the forum, and they contained the law relating to Roman citizens, *ius civile.* For three hundred years the Twelve Tables were interpreted, and the new situations which arose as Rome grew were met by logical deductions expanding the laws, or by legal fictions which kept the letter and enlarged the spirit. Less than a hundred years after the publication of the Twelve Tables a special magistrate was appointed to relieve the consuls of their judicial powers. He was the praetor. In 242 B.C. another praetor was appointed to deal specially with relations between citizens and foreigners; he was called the *praetor peregrinus*. At later dates the number was increased.

Now it must be noted (i) that the praetor was above the law, (ii) that the fact that foreigners (Italians were foreigners) and Roman citizens did business together and were ready to refer disputes to the *praetor peregrinus* presupposed some likeness between the Roman and the foreign conceptions of law, though not enough to make a special judge unnecessary, (iii) that the *praetor urbanus* and the *praetor peregrinus* were required to publish at the beginning of their year of office a statement of the rules (*edictum*) which would guide them in their interpretation of the law of the Twelve Tables, (iv) that the praetors were elected by popular vote and were not necessarily lawyers, though knowledge of law became increasingly a qualification for office. But it is a feature of Roman public life that all holders of office sought advice; the Emperors later similarly sought advice. On these things hangs much of the strength of Roman law.

The praetor was above the law. He could not annul the existing law of the Twelve Tables, but by the framing of his edict and by his day-to-day decisions he could supplement it, or he could reform it by granting remedial relief; the law stood, but he could make a way round. The *praetor peregrinus* had to deal with foreigners not bound by Roman law; his task was to create out of the customs of Romans and the customs of foreigners a law acceptable to both. It was likely to be wider in scope and less bound by local or national traditions; it had to satisfy men as men, not men as citizens of this or that state. The *praetor urbanus* thus built up the law of citizens, *ius civile*; the *praetor peregrinus*, who would draw on the *ius civile* but would enlarge it by non-Roman law, built up the 'law of the nations', *ius gentium*.

The praetor was appointed annually. It was therefore convenient for him to take over the edict of his predecessor, if he wished; but he could adapt it at the outset, and he could enlarge or modify it during his office. It was in a state of perpetual growth; it was alive: 'edictal law is the living voice (*viva vox*) of the civil law'. Fresh minds were constantly at work on it.

In course of time Romans and Italians had more to do with one another, till in 89 B.C. all Italians were made Roman citizens. But hitherto they had come under the *ius gentium*, administered by the *praetor peregrinus*, which was wider and more equitable than the citizens' law; and the citizens had learned something of the nature of the *ius gentium*. So Italians, when they became citizens, were not likely to accept anything less wide, and existing Roman citizens were ready to accept something wider. The result was that by a gradual process the civil law approached the wider law of the nations. But of course citizenship involved much that was refused to foreigners: and the superseding of civil law by *ius gentium* did not take place till the second and third centuries A.D.

Meantime, the provincial governor also issued his edict to run in his province. He had held office in Rome and he knew something of law. He studied the edict of his predecessor, and modified it in the light of his experience. He had to take into account local custom and prejudice, the habits of mind of his provincials; yet Roman notions of law and order must prevail. He might pass to another province where conditions would be different. He must make the right adjustments in his attitude, taking local differences into account. Yet Roman notions of law and order must prevail. And, when he came back to take his place in the Senate, his experience was worth much; a council of state composed of men with such experience has indeed been rare in history.

We have reached 89 B.C., and the answer to our question must take note of these points: (i) the expansion of Rome and the growth of foreign trade and relations brought into being the conception of a 'law of nations', and necessitated its expression in concrete form; (ii) this law affected and eventually superseded the older 'law of the citizens'; (iii) the process of development implied in (i) and (ii) was made possible by the device of 'edictal law', the 'living voice'; development was not stunted or delayed, but was initiated by a magistrate, himself above the law. So far, then, we have (a) a capacity for change and development, (b) a conception of law which takes account of men as men, and not only of citizens under a national law.

We now pass to the period of the Empire, though we shall glance back to the Republic. Under the Republic (except during the last years) the Senate's decisions were not law, but were only recommendations to the popular assembly. Under the early Empire the law-making powers of the popular assemblies were virtually transferred to the Senate. From the reign of Tiberius to Septimius Severus the Senate made law, though only such law as the Emperor approved. The edictal law of the praetor con-

tinued to grow. But in the reign of Hadrian it was con-
solidated and codified and came to an end. With the age
of the Antonines, the Emperor's legislative power superseded all else. His 'edict' was a general ordinance; his
'decree' was a judgement in a suit submitted to him; his
'rescript' was his opinion on a point of law. All of them
made law.

Thus the whole tendency was to concentrate law-
making power in the Emperor's hands. The 'living voice'
of edictal law was silenced; the Senate was subservient.
The distinction between civil law and the law of nations
was (for practical purposes) obliterated when Caracalla
bestowed citizenship on the Roman world in A.D. 212.
Yet the period from Trajan to Septimius Severus, that is,
the period when law-making power is increasingly concentrated in the Emperor's hands, is the age of Classical
Roman Law, the age in which two of the influences which
transformed it into a timeless world law were most potent.
These influences came from (i) the jurisconsults; (ii)
philosophy.

During the last seventy years or so of the Republic the
study of law was earnestly pursued by a number of able
and educated men, most of whom brought to their studies
a practical experience of office at home and of administration in the provinces. Some were actively engaged in
practice in the law-courts, others were men of letters who
wrote upon legal subjects. They were 'skilled in the law',
iurisprudentes or *iurisconsulti*. In an age when public life
and problems of home and provincial administration
occupied the best minds of the day, knowledge of law was
in demand. These 'jurisprudents' were freely consulted
and they gave 'opinions' to those who consulted them.
Their 'answers' to problems were freely quoted and published and they carried great weight, since they came from

men of intellect, learning, and practical experience. Such
men were Q. Mucius Scaevola, M. Junius Brutus
(not the assassin of Julius Caesar), Servius Sulpicius
Rufus. Cicero himself was an advocate rather than a
jurist.

Such a position had these *iurisprudentes* reached in
public estimation, so great was their reputation for wisdom
and integrity, so great the respect for 'authoritative
opinion' that Augustus gave to certain of them the 'right
to answer' problems put to them, and their opinions carried weight with the judge to whom the case might go.
Thus they helped to make law. They were 'licensed con-
sultants'. For two centuries they thus gave 'answers'. But
their influence was great in other ways. They were regularly consulted by the Emperors, and Hadrian indeed
formed a judicial council to help him in matters of law.
They put out an enormous quantity of legal writings, and
their aphorisms passed into current coin, as e.g. 'Follow
the beneficial interpretation'.

The second influence was philosophy. Greek philosophy had considered with some care the distinction between what was conventional (*nomos*), arbitrary, fixed by
human habits and crystallized into law, and what was
natural (*physis*), determined by Nature according to a
large and universal code and smothered by ages of man-
made regulations. It was the travels of the Greeks which
really started this speculation; for they came across
different customs in different lands, yet realized that there
was some vague and remote resemblance as though all
had come from some common source. This idea of a
universal nature was taken up by the Stoics, whose
cardinal doctrine was that men should live 'according to
Nature', i.e. according to the reason which Nature had
implanted in man as man and according to the larger

Reason which animated the world as a whole. Moreover, in Hellenistic thought there had been doctrines of the unity of mankind, and of the duty of the king to look after and serve the interests of his subjects as Saviour and Benefactor and to bring all peoples under such a kind of government. 'Nature' therefore had its laws; Reason in Nature was their source; and these laws were outside and beyond man.

Now the Romans had already arrived at the notion of an unwritten 'law of nations' through their dealings with foreigners. The *iurisprudentes* were educated men, of wide knowledge of literature and of philosophy, and they were instinctively drawn to Stoicism with its stress on standards of conduct. It was they who began to equate the 'law of nations' with the 'law of Nature', and to believe that the law of nations was a faint approximation to the 'law of Nature'. The aim of law thus was to move closer to the objective standards enshrined in the laws of Nature which were based on reason which in turn was the reason, not of one man or one nation, but of man as part of Nature. This was the point of view of the *iurisprudentes* for over two hundred years; and the result was that in all their labours of making law, of amending and interpreting existing law, they had a norm or a criterion to guide them, the ideal of natural justice, of an objective good, more sublime and more comprehensive than any of man's devising, which lawyer and philosopher would strive to discover and to embody progressively in the laws of the Roman Empire.

Thus we are brought back to the opening words of the *Digest* quoted earlier in this chapter. 'The art of the good and the fair', 'desiring to make men good by the encouragement of rewards', 'separating the fair from the unfair'. 'We worship justice', and in a new sense the lawyers were 'priests', concerned with absolute and eternal values, valid for all men at all times and in all places, which they strove to express in the form of 'equity' for the use of mankind.

But Roman law was not yet in such form that it could be serviceable to mankind; it was of enormous bulk. We may omit minor attempts at codification in the third and fourth centuries, and come at once to the Theodosian Code which went into effect in A.D. 439. This Code was an official collection of the Emperors' Statutes, and contained none of the writings of the jurists. It is of great value to us, for it gives a picture of the activities of the Christian Emperors, and of the social conditions of the day; it exerted no little influence on the 'barbarian' codes. For, when successive barbarian races overran the West, and Italy was subject to a foreign government, the barbarians incorporated into their own legal codes great masses of Roman law. Thus the Edict of Theodoric (A.D. 500) bound Roman and Ostrogoth: the Code of Alaric II, the Visigoth, was framed in A.D. 506, and based on the Theodosian Code, on the Sententiae of Paulus the jurist, and on the Institutes of Gaius: and from it Western Europe derived much of its knowledge of Roman law. There was also the Lex Romana of the Burgundians (A.D. 517). But the Code of Theodosius was not enough.

The great codification was that of Justinian, as we have seen. It included imperial statutes and it also distilled the writings of the jurists; what was obsolete was omitted, and the whole was arranged in magnificent order. Justinian claimed that three million lines of jurisprudential law had been reduced to a hundred and fifty thousand of the *Digest,* 'a moderate compendium through which you can easily see your way' (*moderatum et perspicuum compendium*). But into it had entered a thousand years of practical wisdom, and that wisdom had passed through Roman minds. There were no violent innovations. The compilers of the *Digest* looked back over the centuries of Roman law and conceived their work as being part of the orderly progress initiated by the infant Republic.

EPILOGUE

THIS book began by inviting attention to the sense of self-subordination which marked the Roman mind. 'Because you bear yourself as less than the gods, you rule the world.' In a thousand years the Romans had been schooled as no other nation, and they had kept that sense of subordination. None the less, no other nation achieved an Empire so far-reaching and so fundamentally humane. Through obedience comes power. The great gift of Roman obedience flowered in due time into the great ideals of Roman law. By learning at infinite cost that lesson Rome has set those ideals upon succeeding ages. The Romans were 'a law-inspired nation', but the law was of their making and they imposed it on themselves. And, as the fundamental ideas of that law are studied, they will be found to enshrine the ideals and qualities which the Romans of the earliest times set before themselves, now broadened and refined and made of universal application. Respect for eternal values, the will of the gods (*pietas*), and their expression as objective 'right' in the practical things of human life – respect for human personality and human relationships (*humanitas*), whether in the family or the state or the circle of friends, springing from a regard for the personality of each individual and issuing in the maintenance of his freedom (*libertas*) – respect for tradition (*mores*) that holds fast to what has been handed down because it contains accumulated wisdom which no one moment and no one man can supply – respect for authority (*auctoritas*), not as obedience to superior power, but as regard for the judgement of men whose experience and knowledge deserve respect – respect for the pledged word (*fides*) and the expressed intention, the faith of the Romans by which 'with their friends and such as relied on them they kept amity', and 'the most sacred thing in life'.

Respect for these things presupposed training (*disciplina*), the training of the home, of public life, of life itself, and the training which comes from the self (*severitas*). And training of this kind creates a responsible cast of mind (*gravitas*) which assigns importance to important things, so that, when once the hand is placed to the plough, a man does not look back and falter, but keeps to his purpose (*constantia*). These are the qualities which make up the genius of the Roman people.

DATES

86–78 Constitution of Sulla	c. 55 Lucretius died
66–62 Pompey in the East	116–27 Varro
63 Cicero's consulship	
58–49 Caesar in Gaul	
44 Murder of Caesar	70–19 Vergil _poet_
31 Battle of Actium	65–8 Horace _poet_
	64–A.D. 19 Strabo _geog._
27–A.D. 14 Principate of Augustus	59–A.D. 17 Livy _Historian_
	43–A.D. 18 Ovid – _poet – banished_
A.D. 9 Defeat of Varus	
14–37 Tiberius ⎫	
37–41 Caius (Caligula) ⎬ Julio-Claudians	4 B.C.–65 Seneca _banished / tutor / died_
41–54 Claudius	
54–68 Nero ⎭	d. 65 Petronius _Feast of Trimalchio_
69 Year of the Four Emperors	23–79 Pliny the Elder – _Nat Hist. / died / eruption_
69–79 Vespasian ⎫	70 Capture of Jerusalem by Titus
79–81 Titus ⎬ Flavians	c. 90 Epictetus
	35–95 Quintilian
81–96 Domitian ⎭	c. 97 Frontinus
	46–120 Plutarch _Greek – hist._
96–98 Nerva	55–120 Tacitus – _Historian_
98–117 Trajan	63–113 Pliny the Younger _Rich equest_
117–138 Hadrian	65–140 Juvenal – _Satire poet decadent Rome_
138–161 Antoninus Pius ⎫	75–160 Suetonius – _Lives of Cae unreliable_
161–180 M. Aurelius ⎬ Antonines	160 fl. Apuleius – _Afr.A_
180–193 Commodus ⎭	_man of Status Golden Ass_

193–211 Septimius Severus	200 *fl.* Tertullian
	212 Caracalla gave Roman citizenship
222–235 Alexander Severus	
	228 Ulpian died
249–251 Decius	
284–305 Diocletian	
306–337 Constantine	313 Edict of Milan
	265–340 Eusebius
361–363 Julian	325 Council of Nicaea
	330 Foundation of Constantinople
	340–420 St Jerome
379–395 Theodosius I (West)	
	354–430 St Augustine
	384 Symmachus, prefect of the City
	404 Last poem of Claudian
	410 Sack of Rome by Alaric
	413 Rutilius Claudius Namatianus, prefect of the City
	c. 420 Vegetius
	438 Theodosian Code
	455 Sack of Rome by Vandals
	522 Reconquest of Italy by Justinian
527–565 Justinian (East)	533 Promulgation of the *Digest*

INDEX